BEALPORT

BEALPORT

A Novel of a Town

JEFFREY LEWIS

First published in 2018 by
HAUS PUBLISHING LTD.
70 Cadogan Place, London SW1X 9AH

Copyright © Jeffrey Lewis 2018

The right of Jeffrey Lewis to be identified as the author of this work has been asserted in accordance with the Copyright, Designs and Patents Act, 1988

ISBN 978-1-912208-00-5

Typeset in Garamond by MacGuru Ltd

Printed in the United Kingdom by TJ International

A CIP catalogue for this book is available from the British Library

www.hauspublishing.com

For Gayle

The Demolition Derby at Night in Bealport

The cars grunted and clashed. They could seem as stubborn as their drivers. Radiators burst, engines caught fire, grills and fenders dragged in the dirt. The earth was scorched and scored, the air smelled of sulfur and gas. It was a contest of rage, played in a haze of smoke and dust, under an ancient stand of lights that occasionally caught flashes of steel and blood.

In the summer it was something to do, to go out to the old fairgrounds and sip canned beer and watch Gary Hutchins demolish the rest. That was anyway the crowd's expectation, based on the years that Gary's Lincoln had survived, while the Oldsmobiles and Chryslers and Chevys of all the others had been done to scrap. First prize was five hundred dollars. You could keep a car on the road for five hundred dollars. Gary didn't win every Derby, but even when he was the second or third car left there was enough of the Lincoln that he could weld and tinker and coddle and put a fresh set of bald tires on and be back for the next one. It was a '77 Continental, a "roadside attraction" bought where it sat on a front yard in Orrington, with two tons of steel in it, and said by Burton Miles and certain others of Gary's competitors as well as much of the grandstand crowd to be the best car the Derby had seen. Though it's possible that those who said so were diminishing the man by praising the machine.

Gary was up to his usual tricks this night, positioning the Lincoln at the farthest edge of the pit then sitting there as best he was able while the others bashed each other apart, until there were only two remaining. It was hardly a new tactic and the others could try to pull it off, but they never outwaited Gary. They were too easily tempted, or too hungry for the fight. It was almost as if Gary didn't like to fight. If someone came after him, he would fend them off, the Lincoln's wide trunk blocking and shoving, or if they came at him with speed, he would dodge. Then when the field was down to its wounded stragglers, he became like an animal pawing the ground.

The crowd under the stand of lights grew expectant. This was Gary's game now, this was his pleasure, the big guy in the big car, clearing his engine's throat and popping the clutch, so that grass and mud spit under him, and from this farthest edge, so that the greatest acceleration could be had, he sped in reverse at Pete Hammond's Caprice. Hobbled by three flat tires, Hammond had nowhere to go. He oversteered and dragged himself, but the fat trunk of the Lincoln caught his front end at a certain angle and plowed through to the radiator. A wheel fell off the Caprice. It wasn't the engine flames or the geysering water that got Petey, but the lost wheel. When Gary pulled off, his own crumpled trunk stuck up in the air.

It was the end of the night, unexpected and fast. Harv Furman's Caddy should have still been in it but his gas tank exploded and the fire guys ran out to pour retardant on.

Gary got to stand by the chain-link in front of the pit and collect his five hundred dollar check, from Excelsior Sports, down from Bangor, that ran these events. He was a big man with curly hair in a black tee shirt that was sweated through. No helmet had messed up his curls. The weak lights from the single pole left shadows on him, so that what was left could seem, if you weren't too fussy about it, like shards of glory.

The Return of the Prodigal Son

Billy Hutchins came back from California with a credit card and seventy-two dollars. First he stopped at Durfee's for a beer, then he went to see Earl. Earl was out at the camp where he stayed these days. It was twenty minutes out of town and you could fish off the rock in front of it. The lake was full of bass. Billy looked forward to doing some fishing and to seeing the old man, though he planned not to tell him much.

Billy was thirty-two years old, six years the junior of Gary. He had sandy hair and people said he had a hungry look, though no one had figured out exactly what made it that way. Some speculated it was the cheekbones or the hollows underneath them. Or two of his old girls said it was sleepy eyes. Billy had been good with the girls, growing up in Bealport. Better than Gary, who grew up and married Martha and that was the end of it. From the first, Billy was not going to be like Gary, it being a particular and holy thing he swore to himself.

Earl came home from the plant on his Harley to find Billy at the table eating a ham sandwich. Billy put the sandwich down and got up with deliberation, still chewing, and Earl embraced him harder than he embraced his father back. "When you get back?" Earl asked. Billy shrugged, so that his father would have no way to know that he had come to see him first.

But where else would he have gone? He might have found Earl at Durfee's as well, though these days, as a matter largely of economy, Earl more often drank at home. Earl trembled to see his son and made himself a ham sandwich and the two ate together.

"So how is it out there?" Earl also asked. "You know. It's California," Billy said, and Earl didn't ask much more.

It was the night of the demo at the fairgrounds. Billy didn't care to go. He was sure to see Gary soon enough. He said he was tired, just off the road, but Earl insisted in so excited a manner that Billy felt he ought to give him the benefit. Since Alma passed, and it was now fourteen years, there wasn't much to excite Earl.

Earl could have called up Gary to tell him, as there was still time for it, but he meant it to be a surprise. "He's gonna flip," Earl said, and Billy wondered when his father had started using words like "flip." Maybe he'd been watching too much TV. What was wrong with "shit his drawers?" Billy had been gone three and a half years, without a word from him, except at first when he bought the Beemer and sent the picture. But the Beemer was long gone. Now *there* was something they might have shit their drawers for, Earl and Gary both. Billy would have liked to see their faces.

He went with Earl on the back of the Harley. They sat up and apart from Martha and the kid. In his expansiveness Earl bought his son a beer. There were some who saw who Earl was with and tapped Billy on the shoulder so he'd have to turn around, or they asked him where he'd been. Billy began to wish he wasn't there. He hated to answer questions.

The Derby proceeded to Gary's victory. Billy was not surprised. It was one thing more that hadn't changed in Bealport. Even the plant being up for sale again. It had been up for sale when Billy left last. But it was what people were saying, when they came up to him or tapped him, how was it out there, on the left coast, or whatever other way they'd heard on the news to say it when they meant out west and California in particular, or did he know the plant was up for sale? They seemed to forget that it had been that way before. You couldn't make shoes anymore. They made the shoes in Asia. But it wasn't really that people forgot, it was more that they didn't want to remember, at least not on Derby night.

When it was over, Earl pushed through the funneling crowd to get down to Gary at the chain-link. He imagined Billy was following close and he waved and waited when he lost him. Billy wasn't in so much a hurry and didn't push. "Look who I brought! You recognize this guy?" Earl was trying to make a moment of it. Gary still had the five hundred dollar check in his hand. He hadn't handed it over to Martha yet. Though she was there, and Jerome as well, their greetings more subdued than had been Earl's intention, "Hi Uncle Billy," and similar. Billy nodded at them and said hello to Gary. "You looked good out there," he said. "Hey Billy," Gary said, as if he'd never been away.

Earl was disappointed that his older son hadn't "flipped" as predicted. To stir the pot, he started to tell the story. "So I come home, I walk in, I think, fuck all, a bear's got in the fridge or something, I walk in, I'm thinking how'm I gonna get the shotgun, and who is it, sitting right there, calm as a cube of ice? Good thing I didn't blow his head off. That woulda been a good one, blow his head off eating a ham sandwich. Woulda made the papers, that one. Back from El-ay. Where's the suntan, son? You got to watch for those cancers, from all that sun, i'n't that right?"

There had been one on the Discovery Channel recently concerning just that, the prevalence of skin cancers. Billy was embarrassed by him but Earl went on. Pretty much the things you would expect, so happy to have his family, so happy for his son to be home, half said and half not, because he would not have wanted to show tears. Gary was stoic through it all, making the effort to keep forefront in his mind that it was he who had won the Derby. Gary was bigger than Billy by a ton, that's how people used to compare the two. Gary stood still while Billy never did. That was also what they said, and made other comparisons as well, which may not have been spoken but were nevertheless observed, such as Gary's rough complexion that never afflicted Billy, or Billy being a decently sharp dresser when he cared to be versus for instance the plaid shorts that Gary had been wearing all summer for twenty years including tonight. Gary stood there waiting for Earl to stop talking about Billy. It would happen eventually. "Aren't ya going to give your brother a hug?" Earl finally said.

* 5 *

"Welcome home," Gary said, looking straight at Billy, which he might not have, and which was the best he could manage. Gary waited for his father to congratulate him on his win, the way he usually did, the way everyone else did, coming up to the chain-link and giving him a pat or a way-to-go or waiting on the details as if he was on ESPN for the interview they always did after whatever the sport was, but Earl's mind was elsewhere, you might say on the surprises of life, you might say on returns from the dead, even if that would be exaggerating it a little. Anyway it didn't happen, Earl patting Gary's shoulder.

Gary stiffened and let the world go on without him a little while. That was the way to deal with it. He wasn't the type to whine about what was the whole point of winning, or what was the whole point, even, of being good. He turned the five hundred dollar check over to Martha.

A Dialogue at the Checkout, Big Jim's Surplus & Salvage

It was something like a voyage of discovery, into a terrain of happy indifference, for a man like Roger Keysinger to walk into Big Jim's Surplus & Salvage on a Friday afternoon and see if he could perhaps buy a decent hammer or boxes of Colgates that had been drenched in a hurricane so that the cardboard was pretty well gone but the tubes of toothpaste themselves remained in a virginal if sea-washed state. Big Jim's Surplus & Salvage was a bottom feeder for sure. You couldn't go any lower and still be in retail. Worn out linoleum floors, modular metal shelves, cash registers without scanners, plastic bags with other stores' logos because they were overstock and cheaper to buy. Walmart and the Target were like Tiffany's compared to Big Jim's. Not even the Dollar Store sold buckets of rusted nails. Though there was pride at being at the bottom, as if nobody could dislodge you from it, a humble place but your own. A famous story had it that after the Trade Center disaster, when the towers came down, smoke from their collapse rushed into a nearby fashion store and ruined three floors of merchandise. Big Jim himself went down there and bought all of it up and dumped it in his various branches and soon people were traveling to Kittery and Portland from as far away as New York City itself to snap up five-dollar Polo sweaters, three-dollar La Perla bras. Can you wash smoke and horror out of a tank top? A lot of people thought you could.

There were laconic exchanges all day long at the checkout stands of Big Jim's, about this bargain or that, about whether or not it was rain starting up on the roof, about the Brigadiers in whatever sport was in season and whether they had a chance against John Bapst or

Bangor, but this one brief dialogue is notable for the consequences it would have for the life of Bealport.

CHECKOUT LADY: "Want the box?"

ROGER KEYSINGER (*a tall, amiable man with dark hair, in his forties*): "Sure. Why not?"

CHECKOUT LADY: "Made right here in Bealport, these are."

ROGER KEYSINGER: "You're kidding."

CHECKOUT LADY: "No, sir. Last shoes made in the state. Used to be, every shoe you could find. Not any more."

ROGER KEYSINGER: "Shame, huh?"

CHECKOUT LADY: "Ought to just get it over with, ship the whole shooting match over to Vietnam or one of those. That's my personal view."

ROGER KEYSINGER (*dropping a few consonants or pronouns, to sound more like her*): "Nice, though. I like 'em. Seem pretty comfortable."

CHECKOUT LADY (*putting Keysinger's shoes in a Taco Bell bag*): "Oh, they surely are. You'll get wear out of 'em. 'Course all the talk is they're shutting the plant again. Every two years, just like a clock. Well, that's how they get the wages cut, isn't it?"

ROGER KEYSINGER: "I guess it is."

Roger Keysinger exited Big Jim's with his shoes in their Taco Bell bag, into a parking lot that correlated with Big Jim's interior, potholes left over from the last winter and the paint faded on the lane markings. This much more could be said of Roger Keysinger: he possessed a fortune of three hundred ninety million dollars and was a senior partner of Madrigal Associates, a private equity firm headquartered in Greenwich, Connecticut that in one recent year had been ranked the ninth most successful in the country. Among the pickups and rust-pocked econocars, he found his Range Rover and drove off. As he made his way towards his summer house on what everyone in the vicinity of Bealport called the Island, his mind wandered around the fact that NORUMBEGA Makers of Fine Footwear Since 1903 was on the block. The shoes he bought, old-fashioned leather loafers in a medium-rust color, the kind that if they had a couple more doodads on them, a heel-guard or a more curlicued space for a coin, might have been more appealing to the people who used to call them penny loafers, had cost him twenty-six dollars and twenty-four cents with the tax. It could also be said of Roger Keysinger that he liked a bargain wherever it might be found.

On the Island

Years ago there'd been a successful ad for shavers, where the guy says, "I liked the shave so much I bought the company." Roger Keysinger remembered that ad. He felt much the same about his Norumbega loafers, though he'd had them on his feet only three days. He walked around the house with them and looked at them in the floor-length mirror in the bedroom, as if he were still in the store. He bored Courtney extensively on the subject, how comfortable they were, how it was only American shoes that had ever really fit his feet, how they were wide enough and nothing pinched, how Italians or Brazilians or Chinese or Koreans or fill-in-the-blanks didn't really understand feet. Or maybe they understood some feet, but not American feet. Courtney was used to outbursts of enthusiasm such as these from her husband. She would wait them out with a sigh or an occasional sarcasm. In this case she would suggest that it might save a lot of money and trouble if instead of buying the whole damn company Keysinger simply went to Brooks Brothers the next time he was in New York and ordered up some custom-made Peal shoes from England. But Roger Keysinger didn't like custom-made. It went against his middle-of-the-country ways. He preferred, on a day when he might have been off in the boat picnicking with her and whichever of the kids they could seduce to come along, to go to some store that no one else of their acquaintance had ever stepped foot in or in most cases even heard of and look for hammers or whatever else. Sociology, maybe that was it. Keysinger had been a social relations major. He always said it made him good at business.

And he was good. It wasn't luck. Courtney didn't pretend to understand but on the other hand she didn't argue with the results.

They had all the appurtenances and places here and there but it was this one on the Island they had agreed to love. Of course you can't "agree" to such things, but that was a point they chose to put aside. You had to love something or what was the point of it all? What was the point, even, of being good at business?

His partners in Greenwich staged their groans when Keysinger proposed to them that Madrigal buy the old shoe factory on the coast of Maine. But Rog had done a bit of homework. The price was dirt cheap. The downside was small. He would take it on himself to run the place or at least get it set up and if they didn't want to do it, then fuck 'em, he'd pay for it himself. It was the last that got their groans turned to caveat-laced assent. Their amiable Kansas City giant had laid too many golden eggs. They didn't want to piss him off. And of course there would be financing in place and moments when they could get their money out. So all for one and one for all. At the end of the conference call, everyone was happy, sort of. It could have been worse. He could have wanted to buy a circus, was how Farley Robinson put it to Jim Kyzlowski. Keysinger was unconscionably happy. He felt there must be Americans out there like himself who wanted old-fashioned shoes that felt good.

National Footwear of Dayton, Ohio were the sellers. They were so eager to sell that the deal was concluded in three weeks, lawyers and all. Now they could get back to their main business, which was selling running shoes made in Dhaka. If this private equity fella wanted a hobby, good for him.

Three Notes to Give More of an Impression of the Island

A Note on Geography. Two centuries ago it was called Maggot Island. This was not a name in current use, for obvious reasons.

A Second Note on Geography. One candid guidebook writes: "Crossing the rickety bridge from Bealport one encounters an environment distinct from the village to the north. The worn river factory town of modest houses, empty storefronts and pizza places gives way, along the single dirt track that traverses the island north to south, to a wooded solitude where the signs of human habitation are limited. One encounters mailboxes, driveways, and WATCH OUT FOR CHILDREN signs, but seldom a human being, unless one is lucky enough to be invited to one of the expansive cottages, invisible from the road, that dot the coast where the driveways end."

A Note on Politics. It was a common belief among residents of the Island that the state was playing a game of chicken with them regarding their rickety bridge. According to this theory, the state hoped that eventually, if nothing was done, the well-to-do summer people from away who couldn't vote anyway would put up the money to replace the bridge themselves, saving the state its budget for more voter-friendly projects elsewhere. According to the state, the bridge had passed safety inspections and the people on the Island were accomplished complainers.

Father and Son

Earl was mostly bones and easy to carry, in part, too, because he had some experience in the role, like the bride carried many times over the threshold. By the time they were to the truck, he'd quit snoring and mumbling and was more awake than not. Gary dumped him off his shoulder and into the passenger side and Earl put his head back so that he looked like a chick waiting to be fed and Gary drizzled coffee down his throat. "Big night," Gary said, not bothering to be disgusted. Earl asked what time it was. The coffee, if it did little else, began to hide the liquor stench. "Late, Pops," Gary said, getting behind the wheel. What time is it, Earl asked again, and is it late? It was the morning the new boss was going to be there.

Gary had been a foreman the past three years. Among his responsibilities, as he conceived them, was to make sure that the master shoemaker was accounted for. "Earl's forgot more about making shoes than most people ever knew" used to be the local lore, but variations had appeared. "Earl's forgot more about making shoes than he himself ever knew" was one. Being out at the camp hadn't seemed to help his situation. And Alma being gone no longer got him the full measure of deference he'd grown accustomed to, it being so far in the past.

Gary pulled into the assigned parking place that came with his elevation and assessed the situation. "What are you looking at me like that? Let's go," Earl said. It was when Earl said things like that that Gary clenched his teeth. "Want a stick of gum, Pops?" he asked, and unwrapped the stick of Juicy Fruit before he passed it. The car clock said five to nine. Roger Keysinger was supposed to speak at nine.

Gary might have liked to wash his father's face, but there wasn't time. Anyway, it was good enough. Keysinger would have a lot of faces to look at. Gary would be careful not to introduce him. There would be enough of the others to introduce.

"All set?" "Yep."

By now Earl was feeling pretty good. It was a new day, after all. They got down from their respective sides of the truck and walked in like men.

The Speech on the Factory Floor

Keysinger had done this once before, got up in front of the employees of a company he bought and welcomed them, or welcomed himself, or however that was supposed to go. Actually, he had stumbled over that part, the question of who was supposed to be welcomed, and the employees of the company had laughed, and so it had been a success snatched from the jaws.

It made a point, to get up there, or go down there, to the factory floor, where he could stand up on something convenient and roll up his sleeves. It was what he liked to do, to be almost like a politician. Who were the ones after all of whom it was said, when the psychologists were on the talk shows, that they had a big need to be loved.

There were a couple of stragglers who came in right when he was starting, but otherwise they were all there, his new associates, white collar and blue, amid this old machinery that stamped and cut and shaped things, that smelled like oil, and that he was seeing for the first time but already had begun to love. He loved that the whole building smelled of making things.

It was an old brick mill with tall windows and a single smoke-stack. It wasn't expansive, it didn't run along the river a quarter mile, but it was suitable. Or so Keysinger imagined. How could he really know? All he could really know was that for a hundred years they had made shoes here. The river flowed just below the windows. It, too, he imagined, used to smell of oil, but the EPA had cleaned it up, maybe or maybe not at the cost of the mills upriver. Keysinger was in a good mood, as he so often was, and if other companies had failed, it was no business of his. He liked it that the river was clean and that the windows of his factory were tall, and that in twenty minutes he could drive from his summer house to here. If all worked out, it would mean more time on the Island.

His workers – pardon: his *associates* – waited cautiously for him actually to open his mouth. He would probably never know most of their names, but there they all were like it was the first day of camp or school and somebody was going to raise a flag. There was of course not a uniform expression across the faces. If Keysinger could have seen anything, or guessed anything, from the assembly he looked out on, it might have been a great curiosity, or possibly a great wait-and-see.

The two stragglers took their places in the rear. One of the two, the big one, he'd already briefly met, and had heard one or two favorable mentions of, the specifics of which he couldn't for the moment recall. The other, the skinny older one who looked to need a shave, he didn't recognize.

Keysinger wasn't the sort to manage a speech to strangers without a piece of paper. He might not refer to the paper but at least it was there. He began, by way of a welcome, of telling the story of how he'd screwed up the welcome at the other company. Then he continued with the story of going to Big Jim's and finding the comfortable shoes and having a place on the Island and wanting all of this to work and believing that it could.

He had a voice that had a little elongation in it, that told people he wasn't from here, but also told his success. Not the twang alone, but the ease and comfort in it. There didn't seem anything in it that was hiding. It was even possible that he was telling them all the truth.

Certainly his assessment of their industry was candid. Running shoes, walking shoes, hiking shoes, All-Stars, everything but shoes. All the Asian tigers. A few holdouts in Massachusetts and the Midwest. And yet. He was so damn hopeful. "If you have a good product, it's something. If you have a unique product, it's something. If you have a good, unique product, it's everything."

So it could have been a slogan, but the hundred twenty-nine associates assembled on the gray slab floor of Norumbega Footwear wanted to believe it was more.

And maybe it was. If it wasn't, would he have said this? "Friends – and I hope we will be friends, which in my view means we have each other's backs – Madrigal Partners intends to invest in this place. And the first place to invest, in any business that I've ever been a part of, is the personnel. So today I'm announcing a plan that people are going to call foolish and extravagant and un-businesslike but we're going to do it anyway. Now I know many of you have gone through hard and uncertain times. I'm not going to promise you the uncertainty's over. It's possible it's only just beginning. We're going to need a hundred ten percent from everybody. But in light of that, I think it's only fair that everybody in this room, across the board, as of today, gets a ten percent pay raise. How does that sound, friends?"

These were not demonstrative people. Then, too, there was the surprise of it. Most had gone years without a raise. A few claps, a few more, but it wasn't a crowd that would ever "give it up," to use the slicksters' phrase. It was like the beginning of rain, their applause at first, but it gained and it lasted.

Keysinger was pleased with himself. It was a speech, more or less, that he'd given before and that he was getting better at. The timing, the pacing, the what-not. The funny thing was, he meant most of what he said. And, being overall a man of sentiment, it pleased him especially when he saw a few eyes glistening among the gray women towards the front. He, too, had a need to be loved.

He folded up and put away in his pocket the piece of paper that had his speech on it, and that in the event he hadn't needed. In the reception that followed, before everyone went to their benches and stations, Keysinger shook a lot of hands. People pushed forward to get a piece of him or a better look. Keysinger again was like a politician, grabbing hands even as the train was leaving the station. He climbed the stairs to the offices, his office people following him up. Below them, the banging and whir of manufacture began, as if a band had been struck up for their departure. Gary made sure that Earl was not among those whose hand was shaken. He distracted his father, whose breath the Juicy Fruit had not entirely cleared, with small talk. He would find a more appropriate moment to introduce the master shoemaker to their new boss.

The Breakfast Hour at the McDonald's

Of course on reflection the employees of Norumbega Footwear had a more sober view of things. Burton Miles speculated that it could all be a ploy, the raise, but he couldn't identify what kind of ploy. Timmy Thomson had the answer to that one: to get the stock price up. But Marge Deschamps put a hole in that idea by pointing out first you don't normally get a stock price up by spending more money, all you have to do is watch one of the business stations and you'd know that when they all start cheering it's because the company's cutting, not adding, expenses, and second of all this whatever you call it, this Madrigal, it's like private ownership, so in Marge's understanding they wouldn't even have stock. What do they have then, Timmy wanted to know, but Marge wasn't sure.

Still, he seemed like a nice enough fella, Cathy Maitlin from the shipping department observed. And there was general agreement on that point.

It was at the McDonald's that the workers of Norumbega Footwear, who did not call themselves *associates,* typically gathered for coffee and the occasional Sausage Egg McMuffin before heading off to the plant. Formerly the breakfast place of choice had been Chuck & Jeannie's, which then became Just Jeannie's after a mutually unamicable divorce, but Jeannie was all the time battling the lower prices at the McDonald's and then she met somebody and moved to Florida, where it was said that together with the new somebody they'd opened George & Jeannie's, about which if you had a bit of the devil in you you could wonder, given certain aspects of Jeannie's personality that even her staunchest supporters would be obliged to admit were there, whether it wouldn't pretty soon be Just Jeannie's again. So now the only place in Bealport to go at six thirty in the morning was the golden arches. There was naturally grumbling at first, but then people made do, as it was understood that they always, or nearly always, will do. On a typical morning you would find twenty or more from the plant in there, sitting crosswise on the fixed plastic chairs so they could mingle and talk better, sorting out the world's and the country's and the state's, and their own, situations.

Several of the girls, on account of the raise, were talking about a shopping expedition to the Target in Bangor. It's what happened. If you had a bit more money, you patronized the Walmart instead of the Dollar Store. If you were feeling flush, you went to the Target. The Macy's on the mall would be just wasting your money, and living really high. As for Big Jim's Surplus & Salvage, nobody made mention, as they usually did, of planning to stop by to see what was new. For the moment Big Jim's felt like a worst case scenario, a place so déclassé that even the new boss making a joke and telling a story about it couldn't effect its rehabilitation.

Burton Miles was still concerned that they were all going to get flimflammed, that there had to be a catch in it somewhere. Burton tugged on the cottony tufts of his goatee, as he did when he was concerned, and gave his own son Mikey as an example. Mikey was what people of the community formerly called and again more recently called – because it was what everybody was calling everybody these days, with the kids and on TV and so on – retarded. In the middle, between formerly and the present, there had been some more professional-sounding terms with more syllables for Mikey's situation, but Burton had never been much for professional-sounding terms, on account of what he believed to be the slipperiness of their application, which could be proved, in his opinion, by the evolution of exactly the word "retarded," which according to the Wikipedia had been a professional term itself when it started out. In Burton's view, Mikey was simply a good deal slow in catching on to things, which hardly made him unique. And wouldn't Mikey be the first to get the axe, if they were going to try to make up all those ten percent raises?

You could say it was like robbing Peter to pay Paul, Burton said. Martha Hutchins said don't be jumping to conclusions, which was something she felt Burton, who was known in his spare time when he wasn't at work or looking after Mikey to be a member of a group called the Winter Patriots that held certain views that the FBI might not agree with, often did.

These conversations seldom reached conclusions. It was more like "to be continued tomorrow." At a quarter to eight, people would start shuffling out into their pickups and rustbuckets. The plant was right down the river road. One thing about the McDonald's, since you paid at the time of putting in your order, you didn't have to factor in any long waits at the end when everybody would want to pay at once.

Peggy Eaton had the last word this day, as it seemed she often did. Peggy seemed to like having the last word, as she would sit there without a comment for an hour, listening to every foolish thing, at regular intervals taking off her granny glasses to de-fog them when there wasn't any discernable fog but just in case there might be a smidge of it, and at the very end, when you weren't expecting it except that of course you fifty percent were because it was Peg, would come out with the thing that she felt would pretty well sum up the situation. Peggy could almost have been considered the town historian. Bealport had no official town historian, but Peggy was the one you could count on to remember the names of all the old high school teachers and what rooms they taught in and even the years of their retirement. She could do the same with every shop that used to be in town. And so Peggy wound up her wisdom and said: "It's like Miss Brandt said about Henry Ford. He wanted to pay his workers enough so they could buy the Model T's. It's the same thing." Miss Brandt was everybody's old history teacher, if by "everybody" you meant those who'd stayed in school through the tenth grade, which in fact was a sizable majority, though the educational achievement couldn't be said to have made that much of a difference in how people wound up in the economic sphere.

So Roger Keysinger was like Henry Ford. Even Burton Miles liked that one. It put a little context to the situation. A certain amount of doubt was dispelled.

As for Miss Brandt, what a sweet thing it was, and people understood it as such, that in a town like Bealport the history teacher of decades previous could be remembered. You could mention such a name and it would call up memories, and take your mind off current concerns.

A Day's Work for a Day's Pay

Or, How a Shoe Was Made In Bealport.

The cutters came first. These were mostly the women, although if you asked anyone at the plant why this was so, they would have been hard put for an answer. Because the girls had the eye for it? Because it was lighter work? But there were later steps that also needed an eye and as for the "lighter work," who could say? It was all light work or heavy, depending on your attitude, and for all of it you stood all day and bent over something or sat all day and bent over something and there were machines that could cut to the bone or eat a finger.

The cutters studied the skins that came in as if they were maps of hidden treasure and found the parts most suitable and put the various dies over them that would show where to cut, for this piece or that piece. For some of the shoes there could be forty different pieces. The cutting itself could be manual or you could pop the leather into the slicer and the slicer would work around the die and most of the time it was as good as by hand. Dot Bowden could cut a thousand feet of shoe leather in a day; most of the others, somewhat less.

Once all the leather was cut, the cutter herself delivered the various cut pieces to the fitting department, which was the enhancement of a name given to the sewers, who didn't like being called sewers because if you spelled it out it looked just the same as the under-appreciated conveniences that carried your wastewater away, but on the other hand they didn't like "seamstress" any better. The sewers, like the cutters, were chiefly from the women, and there was an occasional banter that went on, between the cutters and the sewers, as to which job required the greater skills, and which entailed the harder work, and overall which was more important. A contingent of sewers would first inspect the leather parts and mark them so the others would know where to sew and what went with what. A second group would do the skiving, which was the thinning down of the edges of the leather so that when it was sewn it wouldn't all bunch up. The chief skiver for the past several years had been Con Bowden, who made it a point whenever he was needled about it to say how much he liked working with the ladies, how in point of fact they were a lot more congenial and told filthier jokes than whichever jerkballs he happened to be drinking with at the moment.

After the skiving, the sewing proper took place, several sewers working nonstop, on the single needle machines and double needle machines, until the parts of the upper were put together. What you would have at this stage would be an almost recognizable shoe, however with the entire bottom of it missing, a car without the wheels or a floor. To begin to rectify this, one final sewer was dedicated to cutting heavier pieces of leather, to the exact size of shoe desired, and these heavier pieces would become the part of the shoe that the eventual wearer would most immediately step on, called the insole, to which the upper, in the next phase of manufacture, would be attached.

Among the sewers were Martha Hutchins (seventeen years on the job as of the date that Roger Keysinger came to the factory floor); Dawn Smith (nine years); Marge Deschamps (twenty-two years) and Bev Miles (sixteen years).

Finally, or close to finally, the shoe in a state you might call embryonic would arrive at the finishing department. This department had as many personnel as the cutters and sewers combined, and it was where the men mostly worked, though under the enlightened leadership of Gary Hutchins (as some in his department were known to waggishly observe) it was no longer exclusively the men. Integration integration everywhere and not a drop to drink, was how Earl Hutchins was inclined to put it. The finishing department was in charge of the lasting process, in addition to other steps. The first thing that had to be done on a shoe's arrival in the department was to choose the proper last, by size and width and the like, from the hundreds set out, waiting patiently for the call as it were, on the metal racks that lined one entire wall of the factory floor. These lasts, of hardwood and a lot of them ancient, were like the patrimony of Norumbega Footwear. To certain of the employees such as Earl, the oldest of the old-timers, they could feel almost alive, bearing memories, as if each of them had been imagined with a living foot in mind. Which of course was the approximate idea, to have a substitute foot to build a shoe around. After the proper last was selected, and so as to minimize later errors, the size of the shoe was stamped on the insole. Then a pliable tape was placed around the bottom of the insole and with this tape the insole attached temporarily to the last.

The next steps may best be imagined as where everything came together. The upper was put in a steamer to soften the leather, then one of the finishers would take an oversized pliers and pull it down around the last and attach it to the insole.

Then shrink wrap, an innovation as highly prized as the satellite TV by any number of Bealport's residents on account of its use as cheap winter boat storage, was stretched and heated over the entire shoe to protect it during the remaining stages of production.

Finally a leather strip, called the welt, was applied around the shoe, at the point where the upper overlapped and attached to the insole (see previous steps). A final piece of leather, tough and durable, would then be trimmed. This piece would provide the so-called outsole, or bottom sole, and it too, after its trim, would be sewn to the welt. In the end, the welt held everything together, upper, insole, and outsole. The welt was like the single family member with whom every other family member had to get along if the whole thing was going to work.

Now a heel would be glued and nailed onto the outsole.

Then finishing touches: any rough spots brushed out of the welt and outsole; the edges of the outsole dyed to provide proper match or contrast to the upper; the shrink-wrap removed; the entire shoe buffed for finish and shine; and at last the shoe left to sit in its last overnight, in a process akin to letting beef hang, so that the shoe might settle closer to the last and achieve the natural, comfortable fit so appreciated by Roger Keysinger.

In this manner, six hundred pairs of shoes a day were manufactured at Norumbega Footwear. Each pair of shoes was perhaps touched by forty pairs of hands.

Among the workers in the finishing department not previously mentioned were Pete Hammond (seven years on the job as of the date that Roger Keysinger came to the factory floor); Charlie Russell (nineteen years); and the master shoemaker himself, who in consequence of the balance of value he created between skills and knowledge on the one hand and his obvious derelictions on the other, had for some time been kept in his son's department under his son's watchful care (thirty-seven years).

One more department needs be mentioned: shipping. On the morning after its rest, each shoe would be deprived of its antique last, given a hand polish with a soft cotton cloth, placed with tissue paper in a NORUMBEGA Makers of Fine Footwear Since 1903 box, and delivered to an inventory shelf in the shipping department. From the high rows of inventory shelves, as wholesale orders arrived, those of the shipping department, headed by Burton Miles, would pull down the shoes needed to fill the order, construct an appropriate shipping box, and complete the United Parcel paperwork.

Among the members of the shipping department was Burton's son Mikey, who was charged with putting shipping boxes together. Burton worked extensively with his son to make sure that his boxes were as good as or in fact even a little bit better, a little bit sturdier, a little bit more squared away, than anybody else's boxes in the department, even if they took somewhat longer to construct.

All of the processes indicated above required each worker to make the same gestures, use the same muscles, stand by the same machine or two machines or three, apply the same logic and expect the same or similar results hundreds of times an hour, sometimes thousands of times a day. No one much complained about this. None expected to live life for free. To the best they were able, most of them found such interest as they could in doing the best job they could, and an undoubted pride attached to making a fine loafer. But such willingness to play the game sat side by side and often in uneasy conjunction with boredom, distraction, long breaks, internet shopping, internet porn, injuries, fatigue, premature aging, and in certain instances an observable amount of prescription or other drug abuse, on the job as well as off.

There are those who say that a worker must have a day's pay for a day's work. But if you'd asked on the factory floor in Bealport about that old phrase, most would probably, while hardly noticing, have turned it around and said the reverse, it being unclear if there was any difference in the meaning.

The Dance in Augusta

The art of the dance as it was explained to Marylou, her stage name, when she first took the job was not to bump and grind so close that the fella in question lost control of himself, but on the other hand close enough that he had the idea that he would like to lose control of himself and would keep paying for more dances against that possibility. That was the first principle, which perhaps to a degree corresponded with the classic law of physics which states that a body in motion tends to stay in motion. The second principle was, that when you figured the fella was pretty soon going to run out of money, then it was up to you and your own principles how to proceed, but in all events you wouldn't want it to wind up costing you any dry cleaning bills. There is no known Newtonian law to which this second principle corresponded.

And thank God for that. She had been working for three months at the Shady Lady. It was a slow afternoon. Was it proper to call this guy sunk back in the velvet plush armchair with the broad arms so that you could sit on them her client or her prey? As long as the music lasted, they said nothing to each other. It was a transaction like any other. She liked the word "transaction," for the delicacy of its veil, and it was possible that he did too. It told you nothing, this word "transaction," it was as neutral as the cash machine in the corner of the black-curtained room. Moreover it was a word that shut its eyes and saw no evil. Her naked leg pierced the open vee of his khaki pants and found the warmth at the apex. She rubbed her knee up and down at the apex and did the tittie thing and shook her hair as if she meant it. The tittie thing of course had variables. She rubbed them together, she pulled back her bra, she saved some other things for later. Their eyes met, hers were dark and his were wide. He thought to smile, to show approval, but then thought better of it, as approval might be a lie. Not that he didn't approve but that it wasn't what he really wanted to say. What he really wanted to say was nothing, but only stare, over her breasts, at her eyes, as if taking in a landscape where the foreground and background meant everything to each other. To take in both at once, or if you did want to smile and be silly about it, both of both at once. But he didn't want to smile.

Now she sat astride one of his legs and fell back as if into his arms, her hair brushing his eyes and mouth.

Now she turned fully around and bent forward and her G-string met his apex and rubbed it ever more efficiently. But when he thrust forward, she pulled away. Then the music was over, whatever it was. It was impossible to know what the song was, even when you'd heard it a hundred times. That's how nondescript it was. They chose the songs not because they were musical but because they were short. "Another?" she asked. "Another," he said, and fumbled for a ten-dollar bill.

The same transaction three times more, ten-dollar bills times four. As the songs took their course, she wrapped her breasts around his nose and flicked her hand across his pants and sat on him and rubbed some more. As the fourth dance came to an end, she opened his fly and put her mouth there. When she was done, he laughed and rearranged himself and put his wire-rimmed glasses that he'd removed back on and gave her the fifth ten-dollar bill.

He waited for her in the parking lot. She was in her jeans and a jacket now and her crazy makeup stood out against the day. She got in his car.

HE: "Hi."

SHE: "Hi. I've only got five minutes."

HE: "You hungry?"

SHE: "Nah."

HE: "There's some fries."

SHE: "Okay."

HE: "I love this."

SHE (*eating, dipping fries in the ketchup*): "What are you even doing here? I thought those guys were coming."

HE: "Not till four thirty."

SHE: "You better go. Look at the time."

HE (*again; silly with the words*): "I love this."

If it wasn't better than the sex they had in her apartment, which was something he would not have liked to admit, at least it fueled the sex they had in her apartment. They agreed to meet later at her place, two towns apart from Bealport. They would have dinner and watch TV. When the weekend came, she would take her share of the fifty he had given her, after the Shady Lady got its own, and they would go out for the evening in Belfast. And next week they would do it all over again.

HE: "Okay. Later."

SHE: "Don't do it."

HE: "Don't do what?"

But she didn't have to say.

SHE (*a girlfriend kind of kiss, halfway between a wife and a nobody met at night*): "Put your seatbelt on."

She balled up the paper that the fries and ketchup had sat on and got out of the car. Back to work, which was slow now, but it would pick up after four when the government offices closed, and by eight she would be gone. As much a routine as anything else, she told herself and he told himself, if you subtracted the occasional handjob to supplement when the fiscal situation was tight, and yet it still surprised him a little, and fueled his thrill that had him driving fifty miles there and back. When he was just on the outside of Bealport, on the coastal road, John Quigley pulled over and put his clerical collar on. It would make a better impression.

The two men waiting for him in the parish house were in shirt-sleeves for the weather but still had on their stiff polyester ties that didn't look like even a good-sized breeze would stir them. He apologized for the lateness. They didn't particularly care, and perhaps felt if he were late it would put them at some advantage. Not that they were insecure about their product and its benefits. One was short and one was taller and they both had crewcuts. A Mutt and Jeff team maybe, but it didn't matter because Mutt did all the talking. They laid out their plans on the oak trestle desk where after the service on Sundays the ladies of the First Congregational Church of Bealport laid out the cookies and lemonade.

The plans were architectural and showed the church and its steeple with the steeple in cutaway. The steeple dated from 1823 when the church was the town meetinghouse, and it rose like an austere wedding cake, ornamented only with a clock and a belfry and a weathercock atop the spire, for one hundred and two feet. For some miles around, only the smokestack of the Norumbega shoe factory was taller. Inside the steeple, in the architectural cutaway, a second tower arose, which was meant in the pastels of the rendering to look hidden and cosseted, like a sword laid to bed. But the cosseting didn't entirely succeed. The inner tower looked metallic and gangly. It looked like someone had brought the biggest erector set ever made into the church tower.

SALESMAN: "Invisible. Entirely. Reverend, look and see if you can see anything. It's like somebody with a pacemaker."

REV. JOHN Q.: "What about noise?"

SALESMAN: "It's not like one of those wind turbines, if that's what you're thinking, Reverend."

REV. JOHN Q.: "Yeah, but how much noise? I just wouldn't want … you know, people sing, we have choirs, this is a place people come for quiet."

SALESMAN: "Have you heard anything to the contrary? Tell me. I've never heard a thing about noise. Quieter than your toaster oven."

REV. JOHN Q.: "Oh, good. Good. I was just asking."

SALESMAN: "Another thing. The radiation question. Jim, show him. The report."

Mutt's colleague fished in his portfolio and withdrew a clear plastic binder.

SALESMAN: "You can read it, Reverend. I'll leave you a copy. What it's showing, radiation 'thousands of times less than the

FCC's limits for safe exposure.' That's the FCC, Reverend. The National Cancer Institute, 'no link to radio-frequency energy.'"

By which point the Reverend John Quigley had already made up his mind, but his mother always told him that it couldn't hurt to listen. So he continued to get an earful. How quick and quiet the construction would be. The benefits accruing to other churches that had gone with Aspirational Technology. A promise to fix the clock that hadn't told the time in twenty years.

SALESMAN: "And one thing more, believe me. You'll never have a dropped call in the church again."

Quigley laughed politely, imagining that in every single sale the man had ever attempted he had used the selfsame line. But his laughter must have been a little too polite.

SALESMAN: "I'm sensing some reservation here, Reverend. You can speak frankly. No harm, no foul. But my sense is, when we spoke on the phone, you were a little more enthusiastic."

REV. JOHN Q.: "Could be."

SALESMAN: "Well then ... "

REV. JOHN Q.: "I'll tell you honestly. When we spoke, I thought we were losing our main employer in town. I thought we were on the brink and could use any help we could get."

SALESMAN: "And it didn't happen?"

REV. JOHN Q.: "It didn't."

SALESMAN: "I wouldn't put all my money on shoes, Reverend. I'd place a few side bets, if you'll pardon the expression."

REV. JOHN Q.: "Well for now anyway ... "

SALESMAN (to associate): "What've we got them down for, Pete? Twelve hundred?"

SECOND SALESMAN (checking paperwork): "Eleven."

SALESMAN: "Fifteen hundred a month, Reverend. If you take it today. I can't leave this on the table. It's way too generous. And the five hundred boost after five years, that's unprecedented in our industry. Hey, I'm not here to advise you. You're a free man. I'm sure you've consulted your parishioners. But there are other places we can go. Slightly less convenient but we can go there. Corey Baptist would be salivating to get a cell phone tower in their steeple. They told me so. They called us up. Isn't that correct, Pete? Called us out of the blue."

SECOND SALESMAN: "It's true, Reverend. They did."

REV. JOHN Q.: "No."

SALESMAN: "Is that a 'no?' You're saying no?"

REV. JOHN Q.: "No."

A grammatical ambiguity that the salesmen let pass, for Quigley's look told the story well enough. There was something about his wire-rimmed glasses that, when he made his mind up to something, they framed his eyes to look small and deadly. She of the stage name "Marylou" had observed this: eyes like BBs, she said. He was otherwise not an imposing man, tallish but not too, a bit long featured, pale in summer, and thin, as if his were a frame that rains had washed over.

The salesmen packed up their papers. Hands were shaken. Provisions were made that if the Reverend changed his mind, he would know where to call. Quigley was pleased that the outcome was in accordance with his girlfriend's suggestion and that he would later be able to tell her the same, yet he admitted not much more than a nanosecond of consideration to the chance that she was why he had done it. He had done it because the town was already saved. He had done it because Madrigal Partners was investing in Bealport. There would be nothing shoddy sending out radio waves between his congregation and God. When the salesmen were gone, he removed his clerical collar and began preparations for the evening.

In the Shade of Young Girls in Flower

There were three girls and two boys. Keysinger was in love with the idea of big families, of the way families used to be. What better thing to spend your money on if you had it? And it kept the race alive, too, though that was something you had to take care in the way you said it so that it wouldn't be taken the wrong way. Just look at the beautiful children. They were answer enough. Eliza, Hamilton, Theresa, George, Mary. How blond were they? Credit Courtney with that one. If it had been up to Keysinger's genes, they wouldn't have been blond at all, and then there was George who was as red-headed as an Irishman. They dotted the lawns and docks and sailboats of the Island like ornaments of success and luck, and there were enough of them and they were close enough to each other that around them the other children of the Island gathered as if to the nucleus of youth itself.

How different in every conceivable human way they were from Billy Hutchins. Of course, philosophically, this was a statement one could easily take issue with. But Billy was not a philosophical thinker, his mind bent decidedly more towards the tactical. And anyway it wasn't an opinion he expressed, but rather what he felt down to the root of his being as he cut the grass at the Keysinger place. The girls were playing croquet with their friends. He didn't know any of their names. They sent each other's balls and shouted outraged insults at each other and said this was cheating and that was, and with all of it they didn't mean a word, and their not-caringness was something that Billy had never known in his life, as if it came with the expanse of lawn and if you didn't have the expanse of lawn then you would always care too much.

Billy of course had the expanse of lawn, to the degree that he sat on the mower and was cutting it. It was his lawn the way in a large department store the salesman will say whatever he's selling is his. He tried to stay out of the way of their game. The one he noticed most was in the black bathing suit. He noticed them all and together they were like a planetary system, with features like their clothes and their heights and their common laughter and their obscure rules that must govern their behavior, but if that was so, then the sun and the moon were this girl in the black one-piece. Not that Billy could know that he was being so fancy with himself. But it was as if his yearning knew things that he didn't, other languages, instincts, secrets.

It was a big lawn between the Keysinger house and the water and there was a lot to cut besides where they were playing their game, until it came down to the point where there wasn't. With the nonchalance afforded by invisibility he had watched the girl in the black suit bend over wickets in concentration, and grab her sunny hair with both her hands and throw it back, and widen her eyes with dismay, touching her face at the same time, and other things, other moments, that were already piling up in his mind as if she were the only person left in the world, having crowded everyone else out, excepting only her playmates, who were there because she was there.

Or that was a way to look at it. The other way was that he loved all these girls, it was the sum of them, the sun and the moon and the planets, that he desired and could not touch. How old were they, really? That thought crossed his mind. Seventeen, sixteen? Old enough, the satyr in him said. And then there was nothing to do but to ask them to move. He could see it. They could see it. If they didn't move, then where they were playing, the grass would remain too long. Jobs had their logic.

Though Billy didn't want to ask them to move because he didn't want them to see him in an inferior position. He imagined his groaning, beating mower as a tank on which he could be riding in to liberate them. Or why wasn't the girl in black in trouble in the water off the dock, flailing around or caught by a stray shark such as the bay had never seen, so that he could be off his mower in a flash and in the water? Et cetera and so forth, you might say, or even Billy might say.

BILLY (*his almost James Dean expression*): "Excuse me. Sorry."

ELIZA (*the girl in the black one-piece*): "Oh. Sorry. We'll just pick up everything."

BILLY: "Not to bother. I can get around those things."

ELIZA: "The wickets?"

BILLY (*embarrassed for not knowing the word*): "The wickets. Right. Take five minutes. Just leave 'em."

ELIZA: "We can do it. It'll be easier."

Billy hadn't expected that she would be thinking to make something easier for him. It showed that everything he had thought was true. This was where the life beyond him began and his own ended. The one in the black suit, Eliza, who in fact was seventeen, began to pick up wickets and the others followed, so that they looked like birds eating crumbs that someone had scattered in the grass. Billy felt a moment's power, as if he had gotten them to do something they didn't really want to do. Yet they didn't seem to mind. For them it could be one thing or another, do this or not, do that or not, in the perfect summer afternoon. The thought of work, or of the time for play being limited, had no place in the world they lived in and that for a few minutes he was given to observe.

Screw all of them, he thought. Screw all of them, that would be nice, but the one in the black suit last. Then banish the thought, so that it wasn't in his eyes, though there might have been a moment when it was.

And if they had seen?

They were done now. The rest of the lawn was his for the mowing. Perhaps he could persuade them to admire his machine. The man and his machine. They stood aside and he went through the last unmowed patch very professionally. One hand on the wheel, how corny was that?

When he was done, he gave them a little salute and they waved.

One of the girls said "thanks" and Billy said "I'll be back next week."

He drove the mower off, around the grand white clapboard house and all its flowering bushes, to the long gravel drive, to put the mower on his new employer Matt Farnsworth's old beaten-down Silverado, Matt Farnsworth's third best truck.

Whether any of the girls gave him another thought, who could say?

The Family Discussion

It was Gary's point that in his family the boys had always gone to Bealport, and not just the boys, but everybody. It was Martha's point that it was Jerome who should get to decide, since he was the one going to school. It was Gary's point that Jerome was in eighth grade and could use some parental advice, that's all, since how could he know what was good for him, all the options and ramifications and so on? It was Martha's point that all Gary really cared about was that Bealport had the football team and Hancock Latin did not. It was Gary's point that this was totally wrong. It was Martha's point that this was not totally wrong. It was Gary's point that, anyway, what was wrong with having a football team and Jerome could be good at football, he was growing big enough. It was Martha's point that Gary was making him sound like a vegetable, "growing big enough." It was Gary's point that this was typical of her, to distort things. It was Martha's point that she was not distorting things to say that just because three generations of Hutchinses had played football at Bealport didn't mean that Jerome had to as well. It was Gary's point that he was getting a little confused and this was how discussions went with her, she didn't answer the question and changed the subject. It was Martha's point that she wasn't changing the subject, the subject was where Jerome was going to go to high school in a year and his father shouldn't be forcing him. It was Gary's point that the education at Hancock Latin was anyway way overrated, he'd heard that from a number of people, they say they're going to get your kid into some college out of state and then it's only the rich ones that get to go. Martha wondered who had told him that and Gary repeated that it was a number of people, including Fox Herman. It was Martha's point that with Fox Herman, whatever he said half the time you could turn it around to one hundred eighty degrees opposite and it would be more accurate.

They lived in a cul-de-sac in a house that was built in 1952. So it wasn't one of the old ones in town, but Gary always said he didn't want to live in a place where you got home from work and it was like another job starting. Something similar might have been said about their marriage, in that they both worked hard enough all day so what was the point of coming home only to start wondering if it had all been worth it. Better just to argue. That was the joke, anyway, they sometimes told themselves. They were both people whose size resembled their dispositions. With due consideration for seasonal fluctuation and diets, averaging out the year, Gary weighed two hundred seventy pounds and Martha a hundred less. Heat in the winter, shade in the summer – that was the old standby applied to women of Martha's age and geography. But they had their good times, there was no denying that either. For television, Gary preferred the History Channel and the pawn shop shows while Martha favored the nature programs. Two walruses in bed. Gary said that once, trying to be jovial, but it went over poorly.

And as for the question of the high schools. If you lived in Bealport, by a quirk of boundaries, you could go to the local school, or if you qualified you could go to the more academic school which was fifteen miles away. Jerome Hutchins seemed quite bright to his middle school teachers and it was felt that if he applied to Hancock Latin, he would be admitted. But he'd also grown a half a foot in a year and was gangly fast and could throw a ball. What was not expressly stated in the discussion between Gary and Martha was that if you went to Bealport High, you were a Bealport person forever, but if you went off to Hancock, who could say? You could develop an attitude, for one thing. People could wonder why you went there. The plant, the team, the river, the work down to the Island, the Hutchinses, the Winslows, the Harts, the Bowdens, the Mileses, the Pierces, these were the Bealport things and people.

As it happened, Jerome was the only issue of Gary Hutchins and Martha Pierce Hutchins, on account of plumbing issues that Martha experienced after his birth. His bedroom upstairs was similar in size and decor to the bedrooms of most other fourteen year-old boys in fifties-era houses around the country, on streets without sidewalks and in cul de sacs, so much so that it would be tiresome to name who was on the wall posters and the like. He was in bed wearing his earbuds while his parents made their points downstairs. It may have been they thought he was asleep. Or possibly they were less sure of it and each in his or her covert way hoped Jerome would hear the points that he or she was making, two distinct streams of propaganda wafting up the stairs. In any event, as was his custom, when Jerome heard his name for the tenth or twelfth time, he took the earbuds off. There had been occasions when he had gotten out of bed and gone downstairs and told them both to please shut up. On this occasion, he only listened.

The Bait

Burton Miles stopped at the Hannaford on the way home and bought three packages of the Double Stuf Oreos. For the last month he had been a leading consumer of these, so much so that Peg in particular at the checkout had begun to needle him about it. Pretty soon there would be a special truck sent up from Scarborough with only Double Stuf Oreos. Did he ever think of trying the Cool Mint for a little variety? Burton grimaced and said he hadn't but maybe he would.

At home he left the Oreos on the kitchen counter in the bag and went at once to his computer, which was situated downstairs in a postwar-style rec room, with a bar incorporating Hawaiian motifs, pine paneling throughout, linoleum with a swirl pattern, and in one corner, its presence suggested if not entirely revealed by a Minwaxed plywood box, the hot water heater. Burton loved his bar and the pinups that went with it and the fact that Bev never ventured into it. It was a fair exchange – he kept it in Marine Corps trim and she didn't step a foot in. Here was situated his three-year-old Dell laptop, which he could access by sitting on the lone barstool.

The hours before and after the dinner hour were those when the greatest concentration of Winter Soldiers convened. These were patriots from all over the country but chiefly from the eastern time zone. Of course there was some sense to this, as out west it was still mid-afternoon. The western Winter Soldiers tended to convene later. It was possible to be part of several study groups and discussions, depending on the chat room you went into and the threads you cared to entangle yourself in. Burton took some care in this regard, to try to avoid the ones that were most frequented by imbeciles.

A fair amount of such were to be found online at any one time. This of course made getting anywhere, and coming to a conclusion about anything, the more difficult.

But Burton hadn't given up. The country was in too bad a shape and even the imbeciles saw that much. You go with what you've got. It was possible that every single farmer that fought in the American Revolution didn't exactly have brains coming out his ears. Tonight it appeared that the topics of interest were the new proof about the United Nations and the black helicopters, the abortion quagmire (where on the one hand you wanted to protect the sanctity of life but on the other hand there was no doubt that abortion was keeping the growth of the most undesirable elements of the population down), and the proposals that were now out there in thirteen states for more legislation to take your second amendment rights away and to distort the obvious meaning of the Constitution (which was that Americans had the right to arm themselves to prevent a tyrannical takeover). In point of fact these had been the topics of interest every night for months, or in the case of the black helicopters and abortion, for as far back as Burton could remember. People had to exhaust themselves on these before they got on to something else. Not that Burton fundamentally disagreed that these were among the chief crises. But you didn't want to get him started. Once you got him started, you could see a fuller range of where we were going wrong.

And who else wanted to hear about it? People would prefer to dream. He couldn't talk to Bev, he couldn't talk to anybody at the factory without the possible consequence of it getting in the ears of certain skunk-livered, brainwashed higher-ups like Sean Byrick in particular, and even his fishing buddies had tired of what they considered to be the same old, same old, even if it wasn't. "Old Burt, going off again." That kind of thing. Burton's chat name was *wsbealport1*. Here the "ws" was clearly "Winter Soldier" and by naming Bealport and putting in the "1" Burton felt he was showing that he truly was a patriot and had no fear in case the FBI was snooping in. It was like John Hancock signing his name in bold.

Burton had about an hour before Bev would be calling him up to dinner. They were eating later now because of the daylight hours, and because Mikey was off at some special class that was helping his type with their reading ability. Burton liked to hand it to Mikey, that he was always willing to improve himself, even if it was Bev who'd found the class for him and signed him up. Online, Burton expressed the opinion that our real problem in Iraq and Afghanistan and all of those was that we hadn't understood the tribal situation. They called themselves countries but really they were just a lot of tribes. Burton had read all about this somewhere. It was typical of our government. It wanted to think one thing, like the world broke down into countries, everyone with their own country, even when the facts were otherwise. Facts were facts. If we'd have gone in and played one tribe against the other tribe and knew who hated who ... But that was as far as Burton got on the world situation. *Wsbigtime88* wanted to know if *wsbealport1* had done any investigations regarding his new employers.

wsbealport1: "Good people, I believe. Putting money in. No layoffs. Intend to keep jobs here."

wsbigtime88: "'Kyzlowski' ring a bell?"

wsbealport1: "What's that?"

wsbigtime88: "Just doing your homework for you, buddy."

wsbealport1: "In regards to what?"

wsbigtime88: "In regards to who you're working for."

wsbealport1: "A man named Keysinger bought the company. No 'Kyzlowski.'"

wsbigtime88: "Google it. Madrigal, right, private equity boys? Five partners. One's Kyzlowski."

wsbealport1: "Thank you very much. I'm not sure I give a flying fuck."

wsbigtime88: "Suit yourself. You know what kind of name that is, Kyzlowski?"

wsbealport1: "Appears to be Polish."

wsbigtime88: "Hey, believe whatever you want to believe. Put your head in the sand. That's what they depend on."

wsbealportr: "I told you, it's Keysinger, anyway. Keysinger is in charge. He looks like a good guy. Put up raises."

wsbigtime88: "Keysinger, Kyzlowski? And what about Henry Kissinger? Awful close to Keysinger."

wsbealportr: "Well you've got a point there."

wsbigtime88: "Just check it out. Typical switcheroo, Keysinger, Kyzlowski?"

The exchange between them was brief enough that Burton had time before dinner to google Madrigal Partners and discover that Roger Keysinger and James Kyzlowski were two distinct partners who had no blood tie to one another whatsoever, that one had been born in Owala, Missouri and the other in Spokane, Washington and nobody looked to have changed their name. And Kyzlowski appeared to be not (as *wsbigtime88* was wont to put it) of the chosen folks, but Roman Catholic, a parishioner of Saint Mary Parish Church in Greenwich, Connecticut. So, good enough. Not perfect but it wasn't a perfect world, and *wsbigtime88*, in the opinion of *wsbealportr*, could take a flying leap, being one of the kinds of imbecile that were wasting everybody's time.

The other Miles progeny, daughter Tina, was living out of the house and Mikey was old enough to be living out of the house as well, but for obvious reasons he wasn't. So it was the three of them for supper, without exception, except on Sundays when Shirley and hers came over. Before Bev put out the chicken from yesterday, Burton unpacked the Hannaford bag and showed Mikey what he'd brought home. It wasn't entirely a surprise to Mikey, on account of Burton's long string of previous purchases, but Burton knew he could always get a grin out of his son and a thank-you that was a little too loud by making the Double Stuf Oreos an event. Of course it was possible that Mikey was humoring Burton rather than the other way around, or it was possible that each was humoring the other to an equal extent. Mikey was taller and rounder than his father and his large face typically lacked expression. But lacking expression, and perhaps intelligence, it also lacked guile or unkindness. He was a strong boy who had become a strong man. Burton had always been strong himself. In the Marines he had been a push-up king. He liked to eat right, or anyway what he thought was eating right, which to others could occasionally seem peculiar, and to stay trim. He liked to think about himself that he had a smaller pot than any other man at the plant, at least among his age of people. Burton was fifty-two. His white goatee was like a flag of himself that he flew.

They put aside the Oreos, but not for dessert. Bev served the leftover chicken with the leftover pan sauce and some frozen vegetables. There were of course women who hated to both work and cook but she wasn't one of them. To cook, for Bev, was to forget about the rest. To cook and to take a walk after supper, on a summer night but even sometimes in the winter, when the stars were the clearest of all. They lived out of town, four miles up the road towards Bangor, on five acres carved out from Burton's father's old farm. Of course the farm was long gone, but there were still the five acres. Out back there was a beautiful forest, mixed, of pine, larch, birch, and maple, though the alders were always threatening, making inroads here and there.

Bev appreciated that her husband spent as much time mentoring Mikey as he did, but that did not mean she approved of every form of it. In particular, she questioned the Oreos. She felt they created an unfair advantage. Burton would counter that it was just like everything else, where Mikey only needed a little extra help and he'd get by. And she could see that, in a way. She could see Burton's good intentions. But the Oreos still made her sadder than most of the other adjustments and considerations that surrounded the life of her son. Burton had taught Mikey how to shoot. She couldn't quarrel with that one, as there was scarcely a man in the county who couldn't shoot and it was important more than anything that Mikey become a man. Then Burton had taught him how to hunt as well. How to do all of it, really. It was a terrible thing even to think, but Bev had thought it more than once, that if you had a big dog but trained it right, then you were no longer afraid of it at all.

Supper was soon over and there was still some daylight left, maybe a half to three-quarters of an hour. Get up early, eat early, go to bed early, the ancestral habit of economy extended to the hours of the day. Bev did up the dishes so that she could take her walk along the road. "You want me to come with you?" Burton asked, of Mikey, not of Bev. "I'm okay," Mikey said. He put the Oreos back in the Hannaford bag. "Take a flashlight, just in case," his mother said. Burton found the flashlight and put it in Mikey's hand. So then he was off. Bev went down the road. Burton watched his son into the woods, until his shape blended into the trees, until the last thing Burton could see with certainty was the gray plastic of the supermarket bag.

The clearing wasn't far into the woods. All Mikey had to do was follow the path, which was rutted and damp but clean enough. In five minutes he would be there. The bugs were out but he waved them away. It was another thing his father had taught him, that the only thing to do about bugs was wave and even then why bother. There were a thousand things Mikey couldn't tell you, but he could tell you he loved these woods. He was happy in the smell of them, there was adventure in it but also safety, it was the smell into which he'd been born. This was another of the things he could not possibly have said, but he knew more things than he said, at least a few. He walked a little faster. He gripped the flashlight tightly. He looked out for animals and when he saw a bird on a branch he froze, telling himself to shoosh.

Instructions to himself. Mikey had many of these. In a sense, he had never forgotten anything he had ever been told. But then, it was only in a sense. The world smelled better than normal good tonight. It smelled of the woods, the bird, his chance. He grew nervous in anticipation as the clearing came close. He knew it from the trees and the bend in the path and the little bit of extra light spreading up ahead. His nervousness and anticipation came from knowing exactly what he was doing. He was baiting the bear. He had been leaving the Oreos in the clearing for a month and sometimes the bear would come and sometimes it wouldn't. If it came often enough and for long enough, then when the time came in the fall, Mikey would go out and shoot it.

Mikey came to the clearing and could see that the last bait of Oreos was gone. The cookies were gone completely. Mikey searched the ground and there were not even crumbs. This was what Burton had taught him, this was the test, if the crumbs were completely gone, then it was most likely the bear. It had happened more than once, that the crumbs were completely gone. Mikey shivered with a kind of confidence, or hope. He looked carefully around, to be sure the bear wasn't here now, close by, watching. He took the Double Stuf Oreos from their packages, one package at a time, and placed them in a pile where the last ones had been. They looked like the kindling for a fire. His father had told him not to leave a mess, so he put the cellophane back in the plastic bag. He looked around again, to make sure the bear had not snuck up. When he was sure of it, he started back down the path. It had grown dark enough that he now put the light of his flashlight on the trail.

The Business Deal

Matt Farnsworth wanted to know if Billy wanted to make a few hundred dollars. They were in Durfee's at the end of the bar where no one else was. Matt had a share of the business down on the Island, the caretaking and the like, he'd done quite well at it and surprised the people who'd always felt he would not go far. He'd done well enough that he no longer lived in Bealport, where he was aware that there were rumors about him and people with an eye out. In the summer he had up to six employees. He'd made room for Billy, it seemed, because they went back to high school, even if they'd not been particularly close, and because word was that Billy couldn't get back into the plant.

They'd been drinking cheap beer and watching a bit of the ballgame. The Red Sox were getting pasted. Naturally Billy wanted to know what the few hundred dollars entailed. Just pick up something down in Brunswick, Matt said, which led to a conversation.

BILLY (*warily, as if he'd been waiting for something like this from Matt from the start, then had forgotten about it when it didn't happen, but now here it was*): "Don't know if my car's good for that."

MATT: "Take one of the trucks."

BILLY: "Rather not. Thanks, Matt."

MATT: "I thought you needed money."

BILLY: "What is it, though?"

MATT: "So you're interested."

BILLY: "I didn't say that, did I?"

MATT: "Don't be an asshole, would you? I give you some money, you pick something of mine up, you bring it to me, I give you three hundred dollars."

BILLY: "Felony weight?"

MATT: "Oh now that sounds very professional."

BILLY: "But I'm not far off."

MATT: "My client pleads the fifth amendment."

BILLY: "Matt, I'm not too interested in a lot of trouble. I thought you knew that."

MATT: "Shouldn't be any trouble at all."

BILLY (half-believing, or maybe three-quarters): "I'm waiting on a job at the plant, do you know that? This'll come as a shock, but I do have some other skills besides being your mule."

MATT: "That why you're cutting grass?"

BILLY: "Fuck you."

MATT: "Suit yourself."

So he did. Billy suited himself. Further analysis of his decision-making process could be undertaken, his self-doubt, his malleability, the flickering of his good intentions, but in the end you would only need to repeat the words "three hundred dollars," which were like magic words in that they seemed to be offering a lot for a little, a defiance of gravity. And Matt would pay for the gas. That was to show his liberality, once Billy was worn down.

On the next Saturday Billy drove to Brunswick in Matt's second-best truck, which had one less winter on it than his third-best truck, and parked in the lot of the downtown Hannaford until he was approached by a fella who got in the cab. Billy handed the fella Matt's cash of sixteen hundred dollars and the fella placed on the passenger side floor a shopping bag inside which were three hundred little bags. Simple enough. The fella had a dark Latin complexion and spoke little and went back to a car with New York plates, which was the one aspect that made Billy nervous, because the combination of the complexion and the plates might have attracted attention. And was that the reason Matt had sent him, in case the Puerto Rican from the big city attracted attention?

Billy never had to touch the shopping bag. After all, it was in Matt's truck, so he could just leave it there and Matt would take his truck back. And Matt paid right away. They met up in the parking lot of Durfee's where Billy had left his own old heap and Matt had crisp twenties waiting for him. It was one of Matt's good traits: he paid when he said he would. He may even have taken pride in that. Then they were at the end of the bar again, enjoying a celebratory drink, or that's as it appeared to Billy at first, when Matt had another favor to ask.

MATT: "When you're out to work tomorrow, drop something off for me, would you?"

BILLY: "That was a one-time only, Matt. If that's what you're thinking."

MATT: "You don't even know what the something is I'm talking about."

BILLY: "Oh, excuse me, I must be terribly mistaken."

MATT: "You're not mistaken but you've got an amount of attitude, I'd say. I'm only asking you because it's down to one of your lawns."

Billy stopped the conversation, seeming for the moment intent on pulling the beer label off his bottle. There were only so many tricks he wanted to have to figure out. And what kind of inhabitant of the Island was buying ten dollar bags, and even if he was – or who the fuck knew, if *she* was – buying them off Matt?

BILLY: "I don't think so, Matt. Way more than I signed up for. I told you … "

MATT: "Yeah, I know about your clean ways."

BILLY: "You don't have to believe me."

MATT: "Then it's simple. Keysinger is one of yours. You're right there. You don't have to move an inch."

BILLY: "Keysinger?"

MATT: "Keep your voice down, would you kindly?"

BILLY: "You're nuts. One of the Keysingers?"

MATT: "Don't go down there then. Do Brownings instead."

BILLY: "I don't like any of this. Just tell me who. Who?"

MATT: "What's the difference to you? You're out of it. Don't shit your pants about it."

BILLY: "I'm not going to tell anybody."

MATT: "Me neither."

BILLY: "The old guy? The owner?"

MATT: "You're pathetic. You want to do this or not? It's once, it's no big deal, the kids go back to school in a week, they're all leaving. Just do it. Or you're not going back to that particular property, ever. You're not trustworthy."

Billy may or may not have agreed with this last piece of character analysis, in that a lot of the time he wasn't sure if he even trusted himself. But one thing he did trust: his desire to go back to the Keysinger place, to be, to feel, a part of that world that in his re-imagining of it now was some kind of a magic kingdom – or wait a minute, wasn't that Disneyland? Of course it was Disneyland. Maybe that explained it. And if it was Disneyland, then it was one of the kids who wanted the drugs and had met somebody or said something to somebody and gotten steered to Matt, who ordinarily didn't take such chances.

Or was the chance the other way, did Matt wind up with the hole card?

BILLY *(muttered, defeated)*: "This is bullshit, Matt."

MATT *(off his stool, pulling up stakes)*: "Beddy time. Don't let me interfere, keep talking to yourself."

BILLY: "I'll do it once."

MATT: "All I was asking."

So Billy got to keep cutting the Keysingers' grass, and to deliver three glassine envelopes to the seventeen-year-old prep school son of Roger Keysinger, who was feeling both a little scared and a little grown-up for having navigated it all, from the casual if friendly conversation with a native outside a bar over in Bar Harbor that led from one thing to another, to the prospect of an easy home delivery. At Choate, Ham Keysinger would be able to speak with authority and nuance about a subject still laced with the fragrance of danger. He would be cool for a little while and would, overall, not worry about it much. Surely not as much as he would worry about getting into Dartmouth.

And what would Ham do with his purchase? It was a question Billy Hutchins didn't much trouble himself with. The fact was that heroin, or opiates in general, were not a category of experience that held much interest for him, or drugs in general for that matter. He preferred to drink. He didn't like the strung-out look. And in addition drugs went against his principles, as a man who still intended to make something of himself. You could say that the avoidance of drugs gave him one of his few competitive advantages, over all the others who used them. And now this prep school boy, this kid who had what was commonly called "everything," this brother of the girl or girls Billy would do what was commonly called "anything" in order to be with, to talk to, to fuck up good, was on the list of the losers. Well fuck him then, good for him. Billy was pleased to have a world he'd briefly idolized come down to crappy earth. It just showed you. It surely did. Don't go crazy and don't believe your eyes. Most of the time the others are faking it.

Arriving at the Keysinger place the next day in Matt's third-best truck, Billy rolled his mower down the boards onto the road and commenced to mow. There was about a half-acre in front and another half down to the water. It was August and the grass was growing so slow it was almost a waste of money to mow in these conditions. Billy could get a laugh on himself out of that one, being concerned about Keysinger spending too much of his money. Neither the girl in the black one-piece nor any of the others seemed to be around. They were the first thing he looked for. The whole place seemed almost deserted, as if it were already September. A single SUV sat in front of the garages.

The kid was supposed to find him. The instructions from Matt were to mow until that happened. Billy soon found fault with these instructions, in that they meant, if the kid didn't show up, he could wind up mowing all afternoon, cutting the same grass over and over like he was trying to turn it into sawdust, and look fairly stupid in the process and attract attention. So when the front piece was done and he was done half-way with the back, Billy decided it would be best to get off the mower and pretend there was something wrong with it, fiddle with the blades, pull a sparkplug. It was while he was embarked on this charade that he caught sight of Ham Keysinger coming around the far side of the house.

Or anyway it was a boy six feet tall and thin with a shock of sun-bleached hair. The boy wore cutoffs and no shoes, so that he was an immediate candidate for Lyme disease. Billy had not actually met or previously seen Hamilton Keysinger. But the kid came up to him, not sheepish at all, as if he were the master of the place and going to give some directions. A few words were exchanged between them. Hey, hi, is there something wrong with the motor, not really. Finally the kid asked if Billy had something for him. The kid's voice was more nervous now. But it wasn't very nervous. It was almost as if it felt it ought to be nervous. Billy fished the three glassines from his jeans. The kid shoved them into his cutoffs. Billy thought to say to him something like, "Take care with that," or "Be careful," or "Don't take that stuff lightly." But if he'd said any of those, it would have suggested he knew what he had passed, which in some obscure legal reasoning Billy felt was not in his best interests. He kept his silence. And anyway, the truth was, he didn't care if the kid was careful or not. Like most people, Billy only lied when he had to.

A Meeting in the Garden

The following week Billy was back to do the grass again. It didn't need it any more than it needed it the last time. Billy tried to think of his wasted effort as water dripping out of a leaky hose. It could leak forever and Keysinger wouldn't notice it. It wouldn't be worth his time to notice it. It would be more economical for a man like Keysinger to just let it drip, once you factored in his effort to open his eyes, to observe the problem, to articulate a solution, to pick up a phone. Billy tried to estimate what Roger Keysinger's time was worth, but it was beyond him.

Billy liked to think of his time on the mower as his thinking time. Not that most other portions of his life couldn't also be thinking time, it seemed there was always room for Billy's mind to wander, to this possibility or that one. But being on the mower was a bit like being on a throne, the lord of the little he surveyed. It begat dreams of modest glory. As for instance his longing to see those girls again; and as well he wondered what their brother might have told them. Was it his secret or theirs, and if the girl in the black one-piece now came around the side of the house the way her brother had done the week previous, would she look at Billy and see someone to be slightly in awe of on account of his dangerous aura, or someone to cringe at the sight of and deplore – or would she see no one at all?

But she didn't come around the side of the house, nor did it seem that any of the next generation of Keysingers were around. It may have been that Matt had been correct and they were all back in school now. The thought cast a pall, the way for someone like Billy the cold did when it came too early, when the ground got hard before Halloween, and Billy even had a moment of wondering if it had been a mistake to come back from California, even if the truth was that he'd had to come back, even if he'd used all his chances there. It was then that Courtney Keysinger hollered in his direction.

He looked around to see a woman in the garden waving a hat the way someone in distress might wave a towel or a flag at a distant passing stranger. The garden was at the south end of the property, as far as could be across the lawn, and it was gated and fenced to keep the critters out. Courtney had put it in herself, and really for herself, a place where the children seldom ventured, though her husband would come around now and then, to admire it and praise her. She was a woman not yet fifty, of Scandinavian type, sturdy and a little bit big-boned, who in keeping with her wealthy-wife station had evolved from a beauty to handsome. Her face in a decade would be weathered unless she took corrective cosmetic action, her clothes were dirty from real dirt, and she had worked up a sweat in the late August sun which lent her regular features a sympathetic sheen of vitality. Her voice was boyishly low and carried poorly in the offshore breeze, so that for a moment she seemed farther away from Billy than actually she was. When he saw her wave, he wheeled the mower around in her direction.

She came out through the gate when he approached. She was holding her hat still in her hand, and despite all her exertions and the hat, her hair had neither flattened nor strayed, so that if she didn't look exactly like a beauty prize contestant, she might still have been the mother of one.

COURTNEY: "Hi. Sorry. Could you help me with something?"

BILLY: "Sure."

COURTNEY: "I know you're busy. It'll just be a couple minutes."

BILLY: "No problem."

COURTNEY: "I couldn't do it myself."

She led Billy through the gate and deep into the garden, where too many rocks along with a small mountain of brush and sod had overloaded a garden cart and bent one of its wheels out at the axle, so that it had become impossible for it to be moved. The overload reminded Billy of an old joke that didn't bear repeating, especially as it could be considered insensitive to some elements of the population and he didn't know this woman from Adam. The garden itself was like a small subdivision, with paths laid out so neatly they could almost have done with street signs, "Peony Lane," "Tomato Way," and with the beginnings of an orchard at the south end of it, close to the tree line with the neighbors. She couldn't have done all of this herself, but from the number of rocks in the cart it was plain that she was not afraid of work. Billy surveyed the situation without betraying whether he thought she was a bit of a ding, as evidenced by her treatment or lack of treatment of a perfectly good garden cart. Courtney was afraid he had formed that opinion. Though actually, he hadn't. There was utility to Billy's thinking and what utility was there in thinking that the boss's wife was a ding?

COURTNEY: "I guess I put too much in."

BILLY: "Let's dump it."

COURTNEY: "Do you think you can fix it? I mean, don't go to all that trouble."

Billy pushed up under the handle and tipped the cart. The heavy contents spilled over the path. Then he turned the cart over so that it was lying belly up. The offending wheel looked like a broken leg dangling. He asked her for a shovel. With the shovel he banged on the axle and levered the wheel with the tip of the shovel dug into the ground, then banged on the axle some more, then pressed with all this strength down on the wheel, all of it to not much result. He went back to his mower to get his hammer. With the hammer he bashed the axle as if he were willing to go at it all night. It was wisdom in the Hutchins line that a hammer solved most of your problems. In the end, the axle looked a mess, as if it had been through a war, with the chrome chipped off and gashes from the blows, but it also looked straighter.

Courtney stood back and watched with a nervous expression, like someone at a car repair who because of the insurance and so on isn't allowed in the shop proper, as Billy turned the cart back on its wheels and pushed. The cart moved forward and the wheel turned. He pushed and pulled to loosen it. It wasn't perfect, but there you had it.

COURTNEY: "Thank you. Thank you. Really."

BILLY: "Not showroom condition, I wouldn't say."

But Courtney said it was perfect. Billy said he'd bring some WD-40 the next time he was down, though he privately thought it highly likely that by then the cart would be gone in favor of a shiny replacement, so that it wouldn't matter that the lubricant wouldn't have the proper effect on a wheel that was still somewhat bent. He basked in her gratitude a moment. She had a pleasant, symmetrical smile and very white teeth, which made her approval seem oddly official. He set to work refilling the cart, which she told him not to do but then didn't stop him from doing. He then pulled the cart through the garden's back gate and out into the trees, where there was a brush pile and he dumped it all.

Emerging from the woods, Billy could see that Courtney had been joined by another man. Billy had never actually seen Roger Keysinger in person, but who else was it going to be? They were out by the fruit trees, standing in front of a young apple. Courtney waved him over. They were talking about the tree's condition. Its leaves were yellowing and dropping. There were scabby-looking blotches on the bark. Courtney had had it planted the previous spring.

COURTNEY: "Meet my husband." *(to Keysinger)* "This gentleman was just really helpful." *(to Billy)* "Sorry, I don't know your name."

BILLY: "Billy. Billy Hutchins."

KEYSINGER: "Rog Keysinger. My wife Courtney. You're not related to the Hutchinses over at Norumbega, are you? We've got a couple Hutchinses over there. Three, actually."

BILLY *(the winning grin)*: "My brother, my dad."

KEYSINGER: "Your brother's wife, I believe, also. Well, good then. Thanks for the help around here."

BILLY: "No problem. You're welcome."

KEYSINGER: "People over there speak well of your family. I've talked to Gary. Solid guy."

BILLY: "Thank you, sir."

KEYSINGER: "Thank *you*."

Billy began to back away. Though he was hardly one for polished manners, native shrewdness told him that it was better to leave a situation a tad early than a tad late. Still, he thought to play one chance. It wasn't great to admit to overhearing conversations, but what if he knew a thing or two they didn't?

BILLY: "You mind my saying? I heard you talking about that tree. The problem with it, in my view, is the cedar over there." *(he points towards the tree line)* "Those are cedar, right, that one clump of them, the real greenies. They're subject to your cedar apple rust, they're the hosts of it. The spores grow up over there on the cedar, but then the wind takes them this way, to your apples, and they like apple trees. I mean, they kill apple trees. You want to save 'em, you got to get rid of those cedar first."

COURTNEY: "I never heard of that. Cedar apple rust. Thank you."

BILLY: "I mean, call a tree guy, have him come over."

KEYSINGER: "Well that's what we were just discussing."

BILLY: "Just make sure, whatever he does, he takes the cedar out. Otherwise you'll be right back where it is now."

KEYSINGER: "Much appreciated."

BILLY: "My two cents. For what it's worth."

Billy left them and went back to his mowing that didn't need to be done. As he circled the Keysingers' great lawn, "buzzing like a buzzard" as he liked to think of it, imagining and reimagining the conversation just completed, replaying his own words and tone of voice, remembering their nodding smiles, considering if he had said too much or too little, wondering if his fortunes might have changed or if he'd blundered or blown it in some way he hadn't figured out yet, the homeowners had kind words for him. Roger Keysinger called him a solid guy. Courtney said he was well disposed and seemed like a hard worker and of course she'd been looking for someone to help her in the garden ever since Francis retired, so what about this one? Keysinger said sure, why not, give him a try. There was a lot to do at the end of the season and then there was next summer. When Courtney asked if he'd be available to come back over the weekend to do some odd jobs, it was such good news on so many fronts that all Billy could think of was the heroin he'd delivered to their child.

The Picnic

It was tradition over Labor Day in Bealport for everybody to go out to Birch Island. It was a day of deviled eggs, fried chicken, coleslaw, Vietnamese farmed shrimp from the Hannaford, clams, mussels, beer, cola, burgers cooked on low portable grills, high-calorie pack-aged pastries that in some cases possibly still had the trans fats in them, chips, sweet pickles, salads with mayo dressings, carrot cakes, chocolate cakes, and brownies of all possible descriptions. It was not a day, by and large, for culinary innovations, although Bev Miles in recent years had begun bringing kale. There were even some from the nursing home who were wheeled out and got onto one of the flotilla of boats. The picnic of course had its dissenters and others who were bored with it after decades and you couldn't get too many of the kids to come once they'd reached their double digits, but on an average year two hundred people on thirty or more lobster boats, pleasure boats, picnic boats, whalers, dinghies, cruisers, tubs, rustbuckets, and exactly one sailboat made their way south past Maggot into the open bay five nautical miles to Birch, which had been preserved by the state conservancy for the use and pleasure of all the citizenry, as opposed to many of the other islands in its vicinity which were private and could sometimes be seen spiked with No Trespassing signs. Some Bealporters, notably among them the Reverend John Quigley, who wasn't from Bealport by origin and therefore whose opinion perhaps shouldn't be counted a full one hundred percent, were of the opinion that being limited to Birch Island and with all the No Trespassing signs around was a little like the natives being rounded up and put on a reservation or in a game park. But you would find no such opinions expressed on

Labor Day. People were there for the good time and, if the year was a lucky one, the sun.

It was an occasion, as well, perhaps, to take stock. The plant was still running. That was one good thing. Or it was more than that, really. It was the main good thing. And it needn't have happened but it did, thanks to the good offices of the fella who a year ago would simply have been called "a person from away" or "one of the summer people," but who now was known more or less universally as "Mr. Keysinger," though in some contexts the "Mr." could be optional. Mr. Keysinger had by now installed a former cookie company executive as his chief operating officer, a man named Tim Vallone, around whom opinion had not yet coalesced, as he'd only been on the job three weeks, but Mr. Keysinger was still the man. He'd promised to bring one or more of his business partners from Connecticut around, and that hadn't happened yet. But he'd promised to invest money, and you could already see it in a fresh paint job on the shop floor and two new machines in the cutting department, and plans already laid out for a retail outlet store to catch the tourists with last year's shoes. And everybody was loving their raises. There were some new pickups in the lot. No additional businesses on Main Street had folded. Ralphie Damone had finally dared raise the price of his pizzas fifty cents, prompting an outcry by Burton Miles in particular about an inflationary spiral taking hold in Bealport, but in general people swallowed the increase and kept buying pizza. And at the Labor Day picnic on Birch Island, especially when the sun poked out after the noon hour, nobody looked worried.

Or look at it from the point of view of Martha Hutchins. In some respects the Labor Day picnic could be considered her day. First of all, it was her favorite day, beating Christmas by a mile, Thanksgiving by half a mile. If you asked her, she would say it was because of the whole town coming out and doing it together. Of course it wasn't the "whole town" literally (no Billy Hutchins, for one example), and Martha understood this, but still it felt that way. It felt like whoever wasn't there was for one day not part of "everybody." As well, Martha was one of the co-conspirators, as she liked to put it. She, along with Ging Richards, and Dottie Bowden, and of course Bev Miles. They were the ones who made sure enough boats were coming for the numbers required, and arranged to get the people from the nursing home with cars and wheelchairs and so on, and got the permits from the conservancy and put out fliers all around so that no group from another town would show up at the last minute and hog up the beach. Martha was by nature a generous person. People always said that about her and on account of it she had fewer than the average number of enemies. She found it hard to say no to a needy person or persons, she would listen to people's problems almost endlessly, she was a soft touch with the collection plate or regarding any voluntary committee, she spoiled her son and let her husband go about his business with relatively few complaints, and for every occasion on which food was called for, she made too much of it.

Of course she wasn't the only one, as concerned the Birch Island picnic and food. In the end there was always extra and people always bemoaned it. When lobsters were plentiful, Beau Listiger's lobsters alone tended to fill a lot of people up. Yet there came a moment every September, when Martha was in her kitchen putting the fried chicken or whatever it was together, when she would get a sudden fear that so-and-so loved such-and-such, the chicken or the shrimp, and maybe there wouldn't be any of it left for him. So off to the Hannaford she'd go and come back and make double of whatever it was, and often enough, double of everything.

Now, sitting on a Corona beer towel, lunch over with and somewhat packed away, the afternoon sun shining for what looked like another little while, she had the chance to survey the day, and there were moments – although not all of them – when it seemed that she was surveying happiness itself. Birch Island was a string-of-pearls of an island with a long skinny beach of pebbles, stones, seaweed, and occasional hard patches of compacted sand. It had once had more birches than it had now, but there was a rise with a nice stand of spruce that gave the island shade and a lovely contour when approached from the north. It was probable that the only Bealporters who ventured into the spruce that day were looking for a place to pee. Like populations the world over, the picnickers tended to congregate near the water. Martha's gaze went down the beach, which seemed like it had been invaded by a migratory flock. One blanket after another, humans you could say in all shapes and sizes, even if you meant mostly larger sizes, lying on backs, sides, and stomachs, with accessories of hats and phones and radios, hampers open or put aside, refuse collected, plastic plates piled, and children tugging or running around.

Many of the men were in their everyday wear, the things they possibly never took off, long pants and long-sleeve shirts. Then there was the occasional surprise, like Skip Bowden with his shirt off, sporting a pot Martha had never suspected in a skinny guy like Skip. Dawn Smith with her boobs. It seemed like she took them everywhere, didn't it? Burton Miles was too many blankets over for Martha to hear directly what he was saying to Fox Herman and old Earl Hutchins, but she could guess what it had to be, as she'd heard it yesterday or the day before, that his online research had revealed that in the case of a company in Ohio and another in Oklahoma, Madrigal Partners had shut down the businesses they bought. There were of course many ways to understand this, as Gary had pointed out, like you had to add up the total number of companies Madrigal had bought, which was something Burton hadn't done. And anyway today wasn't the day for it, except if you were Burton. The Reverend Quigley also had his shirt off. Now there was a nice surprise. He was a decent looking fella, one of the most eligible, you might say, in the village, so why was it there wasn't an apparent lady in his life? And don't tell Martha he was gay, the way people are so quick to say such things as soon as you say "why no girl?" Reverend Quigley was definitely not gay, in the opinion of someone who would freely admit her lack of comprehensive expertise on the subject but felt she still was entitled to her instincts and opinions. Way down the beach,

Timmy Thomson had finally got his kite up, and it was diving and whipping around. It looked like Mikey down there, too, poor Mikey, trying to take it all in, trying to be a part of everything. Martha wondered if Mikey ever wondered, or if he was wondering just now, what it would be like to fly.

Meanwhile Gary splashed into the water all but right in front of Martha and her towel. Though it was more than a splash, really, when Gary went in. He dove and he came up and dove again and it mattered nothing to him the temperature, since he only did it once a year and you could do anything once a year. Martha thought of the elephant seals on the Geographic Channel, the way they went in after mating or a fight. Elephant seals, walruses, if you can't beat 'em, join 'em. Jerome went in the water after his dad, but he looked at first not to want to get wet. By Labor Day the cold water without benefit of the Gulf Stream was only getting colder. Gary splashed him and Jerome splashed back. Playing around, a lazy day. Martha wished it would go on a long time. There was only one aspect that had an off note for Martha, and that was Sean Byrick and his binoculars, sitting there scoping out every extravagant yacht that came down the bay, making mental notes, for sure, about how much each of them might cost. As for instance Roger Keysinger's Hinckley T29R that looked like a Ferrari on the water with its fifties sweep of a windshield and hull as blue as a starry sky, a boat that wasn't even Keysinger's number one boat but only something he tooled around in, took the kids waterskiing or over to Camden, for a quarter or a half a million. With the Byricks, Sean and Kristen both, it seemed nothing was ever good enough for them.

The tide turned at four and the boats started back. They were a flotilla again, a fleet, making its claim, however modest, on the calming bay. By six o'clock, Martha was trying to figure out how to get all the food that hadn't been eaten into her fridge.

The Hunt

When Burton opened the clearing, he had thought things through. It was within shooting distance of the chassis of a 1948 Chevy 3100 pickup truck that had been sitting there from before the woods came back, in what had once been the farm's automotive graveyard, where his grandfather must have imagined he would come for parts, whether he ever did or didn't. Nearby was the hulk of a Plymouth from before the war, but that one was so far gone you couldn't even get a door open. The Chevy was something else again. As was perennially said, they knew how to make 'em back then. Burton did not have a preference for clichés, but he did have his oft-stated preference for facts. They were what sustained him through ornery days. In the case of the Chevy, he had long since been able to pry the doors open and clean the brush and the animal nests out of the cabin, and put some foam on the seats for comfort, and knock the windows out, and spray Rustoleum in a camouflage pattern on the exterior, and adorn the exterior with trees and branches as might be needed, all so that someday his boy could hunt and not get killed doing it.

As the days grew shorter, Mikey had less time after work to come to the blind. He made up for it on the weekends, when he spent his days there with superhero comic books and bits of lunch as scentless as Bev could make them, and the thirty-aught-six of his father's on the shelf in back of the seat that his father had screwed there for that purpose. Weeks passed. The Double Stuf Oreos came and went. The official season for hunting bears with bait elapsed. But then, Mikey didn't have a license anyway. It was their own goddamn property, as Burton might have put it if he'd been asked. The wardens, in Burton's estimation, weren't going to come after a retard on his own property.

But where was the bear? Burton sweetened the offer by pouring bacon grease over the Oreos. He had Mikey throw on fish guts and lobster shells, too, when these came available. There was no question the bear liked these, as every week they were gone and the feast had to be made anew. Yet the bear never showed its face when Mikey was in the blind. Burton cut out Mikey's lunches, in case the bear could wind them. He had Bev wash Mikey's clothes in no-perfume detergent. He got his son up at earlier hours and stayed later with him. Though usually Mikey was alone.

The first snow was before Columbus Day. As first snows will, it feathered the woods with prophecy. Mikey put on rubber-soled shoes and silently grunted as he walked. He was not discouraged, but he was not hopeful either. He was doing as he was told and he would see what he would see. Inside the Chevy was colder than the woods. The seats were wet and Mikey brushed the snowflakes off the corners. The Chevy sat off the clearing by several yards, but the way the bait was placed, there were few trees in-between. Mikey would get his shot, if he ever got a shot, through the frame where the windshield had been. In the meantime he read his comics, turning the pages with gloved hands from which his mother had cut the tips off, so that when he looked at his hands instead of the pages, he thought for a moment he had lost his fingertips as well. The comics were easy for him, as he had a sense of what superpowers might mean. He could imagine doing evildoers in. He could imagine the world divided up. The bright colors of the page were like the bright colors of his mind. And Mikey could read, a little bit, for instance he could read both dog and God and see the way the words themselves played with each other, and if the words played with each other, did the things themselves? Was God a dog? That would be nice. Or the reverse of a dog? That would be good too. There were times when Mikey felt that he knew secrets no one else knew.

But he tired of the comics, which were only a distraction anyway. He longed to shoot something. Reading the comics was to keep his mind off it, because his father had told him not to shoot the gun until the bear came. If he shot the gun before it came, the bear would never come. Mikey adhered to principles, and many of these were his father's, like the gun was his father's. He stretched around and brought the thirty-aught-six down from the shelf and across his lap. The weight of it was pleasant. He took a glove off and placed his hand on the cold barrel. He rolled the gun over in his lap, so that it was like a dog with its belly up. He took his other glove off and his hand roamed the old smooth stock and landed on the trigger. He remembered to be safe because his father had always told him to be safe and so when his finger touched the trigger and made its way around its contours, it did so with a light, almost frightened touch. Then his hand on the barrel roamed and found the barrel's tip, and one finger lightly rimmed it, which felt like fun, or investigation, or, for this little while, something like possession. This reverie lasted until the bear came. It was hard to say how long.

Mikey shot to attention, the way hunters will do. After twenty-nine days or evenings and one hundred hours give or take of Mikey waiting, the bear came into the clearing, quartering so that Mikey couldn't see its eyes. It was silky dark and almost silent. Mikey got the gun up on his shoulder. The bear rummaged the food and pawed the grease. Mikey had no words for what was happening. He wanted to see the bear's eyes. The bear turned broadside enough that Mikey could see its front leg, though still not its eyes. Mikey ran his sight up the back of the leg, as his father had taught him to do. He inched above the leg, a little more then a little more still, as his father had also taught him, but the bear shifted and Mikey started over, up the back of the front leg. People always said he was patient. It was one thing he was. He had waited and waited. He was calm. His father would be proud of him for being calm. He always knew that the bear would come. Again the bear shifted. Mikey could see how little was left of the bait on the ground. The bear tore into what remained and shook its head, as if the bait were a live fish.

There was a second before he shot when Mikey wondered what it would be like to see the bear fall down. It was the greatest power he had ever felt. It might have been the only power. A retard such as he was – for Mikey knew the name of himself – could make the bear fall down. He measured again up the back of the bear's front leg and then a little more, and a little more still, because it was another thing he had learned, to measure twice and cut once. His father, who had taught him these things, was like a big God or a big dog. He had also told him to put two bullets in the bear, so when Mikey shot at the spot a little above the top of the back of the bear's front leg, he shot twice, then twice more. There was little question of a miss, as he had practiced for it and was calm and the bear was no more than fifteen yards away. The bear staggered. The last of the bait fell from its mouth. No sign of blood marred its shiny coat. It seemed to wish to go back to the woods. It went in that direction and fell into a light spray of snow at the edge of the line of spruce. Mikey still had not seen the bear's eyes, except a little bit one of them from the side, and that part of it, or the absence of that part of it, was the shame.

The bear Mikey shot was a well-fattened two-hundred-pound sow. A minute passed. Mikey lay the rifle back in his lap. It warmed him. He wondered but could not have said what he wondered about. It was more like a settled feeling. He was going to go get Burton now, because his father had told him to do that when he shot the bear. Mikey reached around and got the rifle back on its shelf in back of the seat. His father would tell him what to do next. He was opening the rusted door when he saw the sow's cub. It came to the edge of the clearing where its mother lay. It stopped when it heard the creaking of the car door, but it didn't flee. It lay in the snow rubbing its head against its mother's exposed belly. It was the only time Mikey had any feeling about any of this. He felt for the cub and wished that it were dead too. But he hadn't time for that. He had to go tell his father. He got out of the cab and walked quickly up the path. The cub saw him and heard him and ran off. By now a little of the bear's blood trickled into the snow and stained it. This is what Mikey had expected and later he would wonder why it had taken awhile. In a half-hour Burton was back with his son, with the tools to field dress the bear. It was good meat.

The Ride in the Woods

They trucked the seven sleds north of Bangor to a spot where the road met the track of an abandoned rail line. Some years previous the state had pulled up the rails, there being no longer the need of a railroad and especially a bankrupted one in that part of the country, and now the track was a place with straightaways where, with an engine of seven hundred c.c. and a willing driver such as Gary Hutchins, a sled could do a hundred ten. It was mid-December, early in the season, with ten inches of snow on the ground and more in the forecast for later. The usual crew had come along, Gary, Burton, Earl, Fox Herman, Con Bowden, and Frank Magglia. They all worked at the plant except Frank, who had been head coach at the high school fourteen years. Jerome was along as well. He'd been snowmobiling since he was seven, but now that he was older and had a say in the matter, sometimes he came and sometimes he didn't. It used to be that he rode on the back of Gary's sled, his skinny arms clamped as far as they could go around his father's sides, holding on for dear life itself, as in years previous Mikey Miles had done the same with Burton, but you had to be the size of a boy or you wouldn't fit. Gary had solved the problem with a birthday present of a banged-up and somewhat underpowered Ski-Doo that Fred of Fred's Small Engine declared was enough to get Jerome where he needed to go. Gary was not displeased with the underpowered purchase, as he felt it was a way of protecting Jerome against Gary himself, who was the kind who went as fast as he could, loving the frigid air more the louder it screamed in his ears. It was also a way of mollifying Martha, who was accustomed to say, in that jocular, indirect way to friends which told Gary she meant it with high sincerity, that just because she married a crazy daredevil didn't mean she had to raise one. The fact that Gary had bought his boy a four-hundred-dollar birthday present and Jerome didn't always care to use it was the source of some family tension, which Burton Miles had avoided in his own household by never buying Mikey a sled to start with, money being an issue.

Jerome in fact liked to snowmobile. It was being out with these old men for the whole of one of his weekend two days, as if his available life had been cut exactly in half, that he didn't particularly care for. For a boy of thirteen to have control of such a powerful machine, even an underpowered powerful machine, was an incredible thing, one which Jerome approximately sensed, from TV and the like, that city boys would marvel at. He liked the twitch of the throttle in his hand and the way the machine followed his lean and he liked the dips and bumps that tossed him up in the air so that he was flying while sitting down. Even going fifty or sixty, it was a time. And he liked it, too, that Gary thought he was pretty good at it. But he would rather have gone alone, or – in nothing more than the most ordinary way that a thirteen-year-old country boy's life ends and his fantasy begins – if he had a girl, to take her. Jerome's life had not yet been entirely disfigured by the internet, though he put in his hours.

It was cold for mid-December, more like January cold, and light, dry snow kicked up in clouds as the line of sleds raced north, the noise of them disrupting everything but the pleasure of their drivers. If you were on a sled, you owned the roar. Fox Herman charged ahead, running out his big Yamaha, and when he got far enough out there he'd bank around in big arcs like he was skywriting, waiting, almost tapping his watch. Gary stayed behind, so that Jerome would never be last. There were enough aspects of life where these men were not in control, but here the woods were theirs. Jerome may have sensed this, and been frightened or repelled by seeing too far ahead of himself, though it was hard to say for sure what he felt or if he felt anything. His fingers numbed, and one by one, so that he would not lose control, he retracted them into his glove palms, as if he were giving each of them in turn some shore leave.

They stopped for lunch at a diner where the rail line closed again on a road. The diner had a gas pump and the men filled their tanks. It was the kind of place where if, as today, there was mooseburger left in the freezer, they advertised it handwritten on a slip just inside the menu, so that it could be quickly disappeared in the event of a state inspection. Gary and Jerome were in a booth with Burton and Frank Magglia. This was an arrangement that Gary favored and he'd even talked to Magglia about it before the men went out. Gary didn't consider that he was pulling a fast one on Martha. She had all the time in the world to propagandize, she had every day of the week. He simply wanted all points of view to be considered, on the question of where Jerome would go to high school. It wasn't until the pie course that the question came up. As nobody had managed to segue into it, Magglia came right out and broached it.

"So, Jerry, where are you thinking about next year?"

Off-guard, Jerome puttered with his apple pie. "I don't know, sir. You mean about high school?"

Magglia, across from him, examined the boy's reluctance, but also his shot-up six-foot frame and what looked to be, if you had X-ray eyes as a football coach is supposed to have when it comes to physiological matters, his broad, bony shoulders. "All I want you to know, if you choose Bealport, we'd love to see you there."

"Thank you," Jerome said, embarrassed to be suddenly the conversation's subject, which Magglia seemed now prepared to amplify on:

"*I'd* love to see you, personally. Who knows? It's hard to predict. But you look like a ballplayer to me. I'd give you every chance."

"Thank you."

"Your dad says you can throw a football forty yards."

Jerome scowled sideways at his father. "Jesus. Dad."

"Okay. Deny it," Gary said. "Deny what your dad's seen with his own eyes."

Jerome again dropped his eyes. "Maybe twenty-five. Twenty-five maybe."

"Whatever. That number doesn't matter, if you're not interested. But if you *are* interested, I'm just saying … "

"Tell the coach what you're thinking about for Hancock," Gary said.

"I don't know. I'm just thinking about it. I haven't decided."

"That's fine, that's fine. Plenty of time. Take your time," Magglia said, his voice soothing into a lower register. "But here's one thing you should be considering, son. Think about this. This is not propaganda. Who are the kids who get the college scholarships, disproportionate? You can study Japanese or whatever it is over there at Hancock, you can study whatever you want, but in the end who gets the scholarships? The athletes. You know what's the biggest affirmative action program in the country today? It's not for the African-American people. It's for the athletes. I mean, it could be for the African-Americans, if they happen to be outstanding athletes. But it's the athletes. That's one point. I mean, just consider, let's say, you come to Bealport and you don't live up to what I see is your real potential, for whatever reason, you don't like it, whatever it is. You can still transfer back over to Hancock. But let's say on the other hand you're a success. I don't have to tell a kid like yourself in addition there's certain social advantages, if you're a star quarterback at a high school." The last sounded like it could have had a wink with it, but Magglia had learned not to oversell, particularly with the reluctant ones, and he'd known Jerome a long time, if never really well. He eyed him lightly, in a friendly, avuncular fashion.

It was left to Burton Miles to bring up the obscure study he'd seen online, that nobody else in the world seemed to have seen as of December of 2005. Burton himself was probably aware of it only because he was always looking for things that might explain Mikey, like if he fell on his head when he was a baby. Burton showed a particular interest in the ones that showed environmental causes for mental problems, as opposed to genetic, since if it was the environment that was the culprit, it would seem logical to Burton to involve less personal blame. "Did you see that one, Frank, about the head injuries?" he asked.

"No. What's that?"

"Not that much. About if you get too many concussions when you're a kid, it could cause problems later?"

"Like with football?" Magglia asked.

"Like with anything," Burton said. "They do mention football as one. 'Course they do a million and one of these studies. Government's got nothing better to spend our money on, right?"

Burton liked to add his two cents to a conversation, but he could feel in the dampening mood that in this case he might have done better not to interfere with Magglia's pitch. To try to make things right, he continued: "I'll tell you what else would be typical. Ten years from now, they decide the exact opposite. Like it'll be the best thing for you, if you get your brains shaken up a little bit."

At least that got a little bit of a laugh, and a change in the conversational course. "Ain't that the truth," Gary said.

"Pretty soon it'll be bacon," Magglia said.

"Or ketchup," Burton said.

"Or asbestos," Gary said. "Put it on your Wheaties for breakfast."

They went through a number of additional products that would turn out to be gifts from the gods. Fried dough, Kool-Aid, lard. Whoopie pies, s'mores, white bread, fiberglass particles that get under your skin. Jerome didn't add any himself, because the first thing he thought of was weed and he wasn't sure if they wanted to hear that one. But he did grin a little, for the first time in the hour. He felt off the hook.

Eventually the men in the two booths joined up to pay their several checks and got back on their sleds. The day had warmed a bit, but soon it darkened over and the snow resumed. They rode like crazy for a couple hours, eating the snow as they went. There were times when they could hardly see ahead, even with their headlights on, and these were the best, as they could have been discovering a whole new world. They were back to their pickups by four and home by six, in time for the end of the playoff games on television.

The New Hymnals

"Marylou" was over and they were at it again when the FedEx truck pulled up. Ordinarily she didn't come to the Reverend Quigley's place for fear of them being found out and also because she worked most afternoons, but today was a day off and she had surprised him. He lived enough out of town, on the valley road, a road that didn't go anywhere, and nobody knew her car anyway, so she figured it was worth the chance. It was his thirty-first birthday. When the FedEx guy knocked, the Reverend Quigley pulled on some pants and went to the door as if he'd been napping. The FedEx guy, Harold, said he'd been by the church and it was locked and he didn't want to leave these things outside, with the chance of rain later. Quigley had no expectation of a shipment. When Harold went back to the truck and got down his hand truck, Quigley started to imagine there had to be a mistake. He was expecting no birthday presents. His sister in Toledo had sent him a card. Harold unloaded one, then two, then three, and finally six good-sized cardboard boxes from the back of his truck. He stacked them high on the hand truck and delivered them to the Reverend at his front door, where Quigley stood ready to explain that there had to be a mistake. But it wasn't. Each box was not only addressed to the Reverend John Quigley, First Congregational Church of Bealport, and so on, but stamped as coming from Aspirational Technology of Arlington, Virginia. Quigley signed, scratched his head, and brought the boxes one by one inside. "Marylou" had remained in the bedroom throughout. Harold took no note of her 1998 Subaru, which rather blended with the Reverend's 2001 Hyundai. The two went back to finishing their business. She had brought a small insertable appliance, little seen in the area, as either a gag birthday present or a real one, and they used it on each other to satisfaction. Only afterwards did the Reverend open the first of the boxes. On removing the kraft paper and bubble wrap, what he found, in two stacks with a few shoved as well into the sides, were shiny bright red copies of the *Pilgrim Hymnal*, smelling of printer's ink and the bindery.

Quigley and "Marylou" stared at the boxes as though they had won some strange lottery. Then, because she was the kind of person who liked to be sure of things, "Marylou" opened all six. There were, when all were accounted for, one hundred new hymnals, eighteen to a box with one box short. The box with fewer copies contained, as well, a business-stationery note to the Reverend John Quigley and his congregation from their good friends Pete and Jim at Aspirational Technology expressing warm wishes and the satisfaction the company took in being able to extend this small token of friendship to their church. In addition, placed on the inside back cover of each, a sticker no larger than you were likely to find if you bought a book in a bookstore said: Compliments of Aspirational Technology, *Your Friend Upstairs*. Of course the last was a little bit silly, and the "Pete" and "Jim" possibly as well, but Quigley was impressed by how small the stickers were and that they were placed inside the back covers and not the front. Silly but not ostentatiously so. If he placed them in the pews, no one was going to open their hymnal and see a bookplate the size of a pack of Marlboros reminding them of the cellular industry's generosity.

"Marylou" was not a churchgoer but she had been. She remembered the faded red covers of the old *Pilgrim Hymnals* of her youth. The sheer redness of these new ones is what struck her. She almost couldn't believe that something so old could be so new. So carnal, even. That red. What were the puritans thinking? Did they have reds like that three hundred years ago?

"Happy Birthday, I guess," she said.

"Nice bribe," Quigley said.

"Are you going to send them back?" she asked.

"Lot of postage," he said.

Soon they both wanted to back away from the boxes. They took up too much room. They presumed. Who asked them to the party? Let's make dinner, now that we're up, they thought, more or less together.

At dinner the question of the hymnals came up again.

QUIGLEY: "At least they're not the New Century."

MARYLOU: "Say again?"

QUIGLEY: "Got to hand it to them. They must have looked in the pews to see what we were using."

MARYLOU: "I don't know what you're talking about."

QUIGLEY: "Sorry. Yeah. Umm … our esteemed congregation voted a few years ago not to accept the new hymnal that the mother church came up with. It was my first year. I put some samples out. People were *furious*. I got my first earful as the new preacher. Where's all the goddamn 'Thou's' and 'Thee's?' Since when's God a woman? What happened to all the Christian *soldiers*? I tried to explain, you know. But it was my first year. I sent the samples back. It's hard enough getting people to show up. At least you can give them a hymnal they like."

MARYLOU: "Do you think God's a man?"

QUIGLEY: "Don't start. Please."

MARYLOU: "No. Really."

QUIGLEY: "It's my birthday."

MARYLOU: "So consider it my birthday present. You get to have a girlfriend who can wonder if God's a man or not."

QUIGLEY: "I thought the butt plug was my birthday present."

The evenness of their conversations was a solace to Quigley. It was as if for a little while, while they were having them, the world seemed more or less in balance. Their jokes were the hills and valleys. And as for the sex, where had that come from? Life was an experiment. Did God really want it otherwise? If He wanted it otherwise, would He not have made it otherwise? "Marylou" had rarely stayed over. It was only her second or third time, depending how you defined the night. He thought himself slightly rude to be going back to his book, but she insisted that was what she wanted. Just do what you always do. I like it when you do that. So he had his Karl Marx, his *Capital*, in the version that was only nine hundred pages, that he was going through a second time, at ten pages or so a night, because it was a struggle for him to understand. It was another project, like reading the Bible at the same or an even slower pace. You got what you could get and started over, plowing the fields. In the case of the Reverend Quigley, it was his struggle to find some perspective that could explain what was happening to his parishioners. Did not the shepherd have this duty to his flock? And it was not one perspective, anyway, that he sought, one explanation that would explain it all, but rather perspectives, enough perspectives to contain the three dimensions, or even the fourth dimension, of their lives. Was Roger Keysinger their savior? The Reverend Quigley was preparing for the chance, and making the assumption, that he was not. Nothing against Keysinger, that amiable, charitable man. But come on. Quigley was pleased to discover, somewhere deep in *Capital*, that, like "Marylou," Karl Marx had a sense of humor. Jokes about "Mr. Moneybags."

"Marylou" did not consider herself a stripper, but rather a jazz singer who needed a job in a part of the country where jazz singers weren't much in demand. This was during her phases for which the word "aspirational" might have found another application. In her more candid periods, darker thoughts surfaced, creatures from the blackish lagoon, as the one decent therapist she'd ever had was fond to call them. Not that there was no demand whatsoever for jazz singers in the state. There were some weddings in the summer and gigs at a few seaside clubs. But whether there were gigs or not, and whether she was a stripper who once in a while got lucky or a jazz singer who mostly didn't, one unassailable constant was that she had a voice. And she'd grown up going to church, where she used that voice for the first time. The red books were faded then. They didn't startle you with their life. What startled her back then was sex, though that may have been a cruel way to put it, even to herself. The covers of the red books were faded and sex and everything that went with it were so real. Was that why it was fun to fuck a minister now? It could be it was how it started. Their conversations at the Shady Lady, which he walked into on his own two feet and so did she. Where you from? Bealport. He needn't have said that. It was part of the transaction to lie, it was almost not complete without it. Then, lo and behold, her minister was a kind, decent, unhypocritical, struggling-to-believe-in-something, trim, naturally quiet, possibly shy, possibly ineffectual though it was yet to be proved one way or the other, good and eager lay. Did she think all those things? She did, actually. Just as she wondered if God was a man. For not much reason (it was not, for example, a stirring of belief), but perhaps because she liked to sing and there were some old ones she remembered, "Marylou" left the Reverend upstairs on the bed with his *Capital* and revisited the boxes of hymnals downstairs. They had not taken godly flight. So (you could say) it was he upstairs with his red book, she downstairs with hers. She opened one of the *Pilgrim Hymnals* and thumbed the pages. The first hymn that she found that made her heart beat fast for memory and love, she sang aloud:

Guide me, O Thou great Jehovah
Pilgrim through this barren land;
I am weak, but Thou art mighty,
Hold me with Thy pow'rful hand.
Bread of heaven, Bread of heaven,
Feed me till I want no more;
Feed me till I want no more.

Open now thy crystal fountain,
Whence thy healing stream doth flow;
Let the fire and cloudy pillar
Lead me all my journey through.
Strong Deliv'rer, strong Deliv'rer,
Be Thou still my Strength and Shield;
Be Thou still my Strength and Shield.

Lord, I trust Thy mighty power,
Wondrous are Thy works of old;
Thou deliv'rest Thine from thralldom,
Who for naught themselves had sold:
Thou didst conquer, Thou didst conquer
Sin and Satan and the grave,
Sin and Satan and the grave.

When I tread the verge of Jordan,
Bid my anxious fears subside;
Death of death and hell's Destruction,
Land me safe on Canaan's side.
Songs of praises, songs of praises,
I will ever give to Thee;
I will ever give to Thee.

Though she was a jazz singer, she had a voice that stayed close to phrases and didn't mess around. She attacked songs as though daring every word to be believed. And yet hers was a sparrow's voice, she was a little Piaf who attacked. There was a purity of hope there. She didn't give up, even when it seemed that she might, even when she seemed about to be overwhelmed. All of it, all of her, wafted up the stairs and found the Reverend Quigley on the bed with his book. Far from distracting him, it concentrated his mind, it made it go faster, as if she were showing him a clear way through. Don't be brain-bound. Don't believe everything you read. Only feel the suffering of the poor. Before Sunday came around, the new hymnals were in the pews of his church. With their bright red jackets and fresh-from-the-bindery smell, they could hardly go unnoticed, and yet even though the Reverend Quigley's congregants were known to be squirrely around change of any kind, and even though enough of them noticed the little sticker on the inside of the back covers which explained their arrival, no one complained.

The Breakfast Hour at the McDonald's

Roger Keysinger had in his pocket a piece of paper with numbers on it that he knew would not be good news for his workers at the plant, but he went into the McDonald's anyway. It was even possible that he went into the McDonald's especially because those numbers were in his pocket. It was early on a January morning when the wind chill was minus eleven. He had flown up from Connecticut private and been whisked from Bangor in a black car. The black car sat in the McDonald's parking lot with the motor running, as out of place as the previous summer Keysinger's Range Rover had been at Big Jim's. But there was no help for it. The black car would deliver him to the plant. He could have told the driver to take a few runs around the block, but there were no blocks to run around, and besides, Keysinger was unsure how long he would be. He was stopping at the McDonald's in part because he'd been up since four and his caffeine was running low, but more because he wanted to see what his people looked like when they weren't making shoes. Or, less articulately, he felt he wanted to know them better. That sounded ridiculous, even to himself. He wanted to know at least one thing about them and he couldn't say that he did. The people in the front office, maybe, a little, Sean and Kristen for examples, he could guess a couple things about, the two yuppies of Bealport. But the remainder were lumped in his mind, an unfinished sculpture. If nothing else, he wanted the interface between himself and them, the friction, the feel of life. His urge to be a regular guy had returned and he wanted to eat what they were eating. Egg McMuffin? So be it. The Big Breakfast, even better. Perhaps, too, he wanted to show, to himself and/or others, that he was not out of touch. In Connecticut, on the Post Road, he'd been known to stop in at the arches, often enough that Court-ney could add it to her litanies about cholesterol, which by the way she always annoyed him by pronouncing "cloresterol," the way Bush pronounced "nookular." He was wearing a very high-end North Face parka, which thankfully didn't look very high end but which was said to be warm down to some insanely low degree, along with pressed khakis and Norumbega loafers, the last despite the icy sleet on the ground.

It was the black car that caught everyone's attention before they even knew who was in it. Fox Herman's first impression was that the FBI was coming to do a raid. He made that speculation as soon as the car turned in, prompting everyone else to jump all over him for there being obviously nothing around worth raiding. Mexicans making the Egg McMuffins? Not even that. The next guess was Timmy Thomson's, that it was the lieutenant governor or one of those. This naturally prompted one of Burt Miles' sarcastic comments about government waste of taxpayer dollars, but by then Keysinger was getting out of the car, the driver holding the door for him. *What was he doing here?*

Keysinger came in and stood in line like everybody else. Of course he would have to, there being no valet servers or cheesy red elite bits of carpet for high value patrons at McDonald's. You could even say that the McDonald's wasn't prepared for its eminent visitor. This was the impression some of the regulars got. A couple of them, Charlie Russell and Dawn Smith in particular, had the urge to go up and help him out, offer him a seat, offer to order for him, but neither went through with it, perhaps sensing, in Charlie's case, that he would be considered a kiss-ass by everybody else and, in Dawn's case, she of the boobs, that it could be considered, again by everybody else, as a not too subtle invitation to extracurriculars at some later date. Instead, the workers of Norumbega watched their boss with studied inattention. They were not going to be like those natives you could see on the Nat Geo channel who stare at any foreigner who comes around. But it got very quiet around the six or seven tables where the morning regulars congregated. It seemed to make the whole restaurant quiet down, so that you could hear the fryers and the food orders better. Keysinger ordered a Big Breakfast and a large coffee. You could hear it right across the restaurant. His food came almost immediately, as Stump Watkins ran an efficient franchise.

Keysinger then naturally turned around to look for a place to sit. His eyes fell on the regulars who were still studiously avoiding overtly paying attention to what covertly a hundred percent they were. He caught one or two glances and smiled wryly, as if "fancy meeting you here." It was as obvious to him what the rest were doing as it was opaque to them why he had walked into their sanctuary in the first place. They would have been touched, for sure, if they'd known. Or perhaps less touched if they knew the numbers that were in his pocket.

"Mind if I join you?" It's what broke the ice, it was all they needed. People were immediately making room, moving away, stacking trays, throwing out all kinds of used napkins and containers and bits of uneaten food. Keysinger sat down, his long legs splayed out under a second table that had been cleared for him. "I remember some of you. I'm Rog Keysinger?" his sentence rising in vague assimilation of his daughters' adolescent speech patterns. Then, because it was easier than speaking, or because it gave him some time to think what to say, he began chowing down on the scrambled eggs, hotcakes and sausage. He handled his flimsy plastic cutlery without embarrassment, perhaps earning some points in so doing or anyway feeling that he might. Meanwhile, one at a time, like drips from a faucet that start coming faster, those around him introduced themselves. Pete Hammond. Fox Herman. Timmy Thomson. Burton Miles. Marge Deschamps. And so on. As usual, the girls were a little more tentative, until they got going. To each one, Keysinger nodded as he ate, having the excuse not to talk and say the same thing over and over while his mouth was full. He finished his eggs and hotcakes in no time – he seemed to be a big man with a big appetite, which the others found a pleasing characteristic – then asked generally how the winter had been. This elicited the range of opinions that you might expect. Dreadful, long, dark, lot of snow, too much snow, not enough snow, not too bad. Keysinger opined that it sounded a lot like what they had down in Connecticut, albeit maybe a little milder down there because of course they had the Gulf Stream.

A conversation of sorts drifted. Some had their eyes on the clock, as it was already twenty-five past seven and it obviously wouldn't do to demonstrate a casual attitude towards punctuality right in front of the boss. They asked him how his flight had been. He asked them how the deer season had been. They asked him whether he was slipping and sliding a little in those loafers. He asked them about the Brigadiers' basketball season. None of the answers to any of these questions was particularly startling. Just things to say, keeping it going. All for one and one for all? Maybe. Keysinger was now considering the paper in his pocket. Nobody had asked him how the company was doing so of course he hadn't had to answer. But the longer he sat there, the odder he felt for not having sufficiently considered what he would say if by chance he was asked. It was one of those things where he might have imagined, if he'd thought about it at all, that the right answer would present itself spontaneously. Keysinger was a believer in the power of spontaneity, of waiting for a moment. But now he felt that moment somewhere out there. Should he bring it up himself? He told himself he couldn't find it, that the moment which might compel him was still too elusive and vague. But really, he didn't want to find it. Bring everybody's spirits down, right then, right there, in person, and be asked more questions than he could answer? No thanks. Hadn't he walked into the McDonald's in Bealport to express solidarity, or anyway to *feel* solidarity, to reassure himself? Like his employees, he glanced at the time, suddenly hoping to run out the clock. He was about to excuse himself and be gone, citing a meeting which in truth wasn't to start for an hour, when Burt Miles asked, as if casually and without any real connection to anything previously said, "So, how're we doing?"

"You people? You're great," Keysinger said.

"I guess, if it's okay to ask, I meant the business as a whole?" Burton had his hands clasped in his lap and his legs out and crossed at the ankles, doing the best he could to keep a nonchalant posture, as if his question were no sudden departure, nor on a different plane from "How was the flight?" or "How're the shoes?"

The solution finally came to Keysinger, as he had faith that it would if he waited for the moment. *It was a subject to bring up with the front office first.* Fortified with this obvious understanding, this categorical imperative, this fine rationalization, he said, "We're getting there."

The first time he said it, it sounded to Keysinger's ears a little tentative and even weary, as if he were emphasizing a long slog ahead, so he repeated the words more declaratively, to clarify and correct, to suggest things were well along. "We're getting there."

Then he stood up and bused his own trash. It was the least, or perhaps the most, he could do. People appreciated that part. It was as if the president of the whole country had come in and done the same, slid the trash off the tray through the appropriate slot and stacked the tray on top. It showed he knew certain things. It almost showed he was a man of integrity.

Keysinger extended a hand and shook several of theirs, then grimaced apologetically and left. The black car had pulled around and was waiting for him in front. The driver was just emerging into the biting cold to get the back door open, but this time Keysinger beat him to it, hopping in the front. He perhaps did this for effect. For he knew now that he would be watched.

Meanwhile his words lingered. They were enough to satisfy Martha, Fox Herman, Con Bowden, Timmy, Charlie, Dawn, Bev, and a number of the others, if not especially Burt Miles, and now it was time to get to work.

A Dialogue in the Boardroom

It wasn't much of a boardroom. The table was long enough, but of plywood. The chairs were assorted. You could say it was a picture of New England frugality, though perhaps also it reflected the fact that Norumbega Footwear had seldom had a full board of directors, so what did it need a boardroom for? It was a place to store things in the corners and for the higher-ups occasionally to have lunch. Now folding chairs and swivel chairs from other offices were brought in, and bottles of Poland Spring placed in the center of the long table, where they looked meager and forlorn, like they'd been deposited at the North Pole and were awaiting polar bears to come get them.

In attendance were Keysinger, Tim Vallone (the chief operating officer), Mark Brine (Vallone's first hire, the finance officer), Catherine Wilson (an outside accountant down from Bangor), Dave Hirshhorn (Vallone's second hire, in charge of marketing), Sean Byrick (personnel and general operations), and Kristen Byrick (purchasing). If there was anything odd in the setup, it was only that all had laptops but the boss. Keysinger didn't necessarily believe in laptops. Or rather, he believed in them for everyone but himself. He wasn't a Luddite, he was simply cautious. Let others get hung on their digital records. Let others do his dirty digital work for him. He saw a pencil as a competitive advantage.

The piece of paper with the numbers was already out of his pocket. Xeroxes had been duly made and everyone had their copy. The plywood table was littered with the bad news. Production up twenty percent, sales down thirty percent. Keysinger was striking a note that was serious but not despairing. It was a time for solutions.

KEYSINGER: "Sean, did you come up with that list?"

BYRICK *(a couple clicks, bringing it up)*: "Got it."

KEYSINGER: "Okay. Now. If anybody has a better idea … I'm all ears." *(scanning the room)* "Dave?"

HIRSHHORN *(reluctantly)*: "Look, it's *American made*. We've got to keep stressing that. *American made*. Once the message gets out … "

KEYSINGER: "Anybody else?"

BRINE: "We could talk about rolling back the raise."

KEYSINGER: "And have one hundred percent of everybody pissed?

BRINE *(a hasty if sardonic retreat)*: "Correct. I didn't say it was a good option. Just an option."

KEYSINGER: "Anybody else?"

KRISTEN: "I'm coming up with some suppliers in Saskatchewan. I'm waiting on the figures, what the real savings would be, with shipping."

VALLONE: "Look, we're a new team. I'm not making excuses for anybody, but it's true, we're new. Everybody acknowledge their mistakes and let's move on."

KEYSINGER *(covering his annoyance with a facetious tone)*: "That's what I'm trying to do right now, Tim: move on."

But there appeared to be no solutions, none anyway that could withstand Keysinger's skeptical gaze, save the one on Sean Byrick's screen.

KEYSINGER *(shifting gears)*: "Look, I don't want anybody to read this wrong. I believe in this company. One bad quarter's not going to kill us, or my enthusiasm, or anything. But, come on, folks. This is a business. I've got partners. I've got to go back to Connecticut and convince some people. So. Sean, read your list. If anybody has any objections, say so now."

BYRICK *(reading from screen)*: "Judith Harvey. Dorothy Weller. Frank Benn. Charles Russell. Pamela Harrelton. John McBridge. Carl Esposito. Michael Miles. Mary Francis Donnelson. Edward Parsons. Thomas Lacques. Henry Dinsmore. Earl Hutchins."

With all the names spoken full, shorn of nicknames, it sounded like an honor roll for the dead, something from Memorial Day, or an older Memorial Day, Decoration Day, when Gold Star mothers rode in convertible cars down Main Street. No one objected, not to any particular name on the list, nor to the presentation of them all. To the contrary, the very fact that Keysinger asked for the names to be read aloud was felt generally to be a point in his favor. Vallone in particular, who'd worked at the baked goods company and others, a hired hand in the MBA army, found it unprecedented. It seemed so decent. It seemed so respectful of the community. It expressed the proper regret. It made him feel that he hadn't made a mistake, or at minimum might possibly not have made a mistake, coming to this godforsaken place with its endless winters and slight chances. Roger Keysinger had some of the same feelings, albeit whirling on the circular rails of selfhood, with the gravitational force of an amusement park ride. He was doing the best he could. The numbers were awful. What else was he supposed to do? He had the names read aloud as a way to say that this was all personal and small and human scale to him, to convince himself that he really cared.

The Island, January

By Columbus Day Billy had done enough odd jobs for Courtney Keysinger that she trusted him to do some painting over the winter. It was another of the skills that he had picked up along the way, being the sort of local person who had to know how to do damn near everything in order to make one living. So he was upstairs in the otherwise closed up house repainting the two guest bedrooms at the end of the upstairs hall on the January day Rog Keysinger came up. For the two and a half weeks he'd been working, Billy had been scrupulous about not poking around in anybody's diary or photo albums, nor pocketing any loose change he came across, nor drinking so much as a beer from the fridge. It was too good a gig for him to mess around with. If the Keysingers liked him enough, he might never have to work for Matt Farnsworth again, and that would be none too soon. The spectre of the kid and the glassine envelope had receded somewhat, the way crimes and lies will do, for after all, when all is said and done, aren't they part of the fabric of life like everything else? The house was a comfortable fifty-five degrees. Billy wasn't the greatest painter ever, but when he took his time he was pretty fair. Rog Keysinger surprised him when the black car pulled up shortly after noon. Billy immediately went to turn the thermostat up to seventy. Keysinger said don't bother, he liked a house cold.

It was on some basis such as that that the two men seemed to get along. As well, Keysinger had continued to hear good things about Billy from Courtney. His politeness, his eagerness. She might have added his occasional James Dean-ness, but didn't, for private reasons. Keysinger had brought a footlong from the Subway for his lunch. With Courtney not around and no secretary to book a table somewhere, his eating habits were not the best. He made a few calls to Greenwich and one long one to London, then sat down with his bag from the Subway and a Coke. Feeling once again expansive, he shouted upstairs for Billy. "Have you had your lunch?" "Thank you, sir. I'm fine." "The fuck is that 'sir' shit? Come on down." Billy took this as either an order or an opportunity, though possibly, too, it was an opportunity cloaked in an order. As Billy walked into the self-consciously country-style kitchen, in which, for example, the Gaggenau sat in a sea of pine floorboards, Keysinger added, for good measure, "Take a load off."

Keysinger was on a stool by the center island. He started to cut his sub in half. "Too big for me." "No, really, sir," Billy protested. "Don't know why I ordered it," Keysinger continued.

Billy didn't want to be rude, rudeness itself not being the issue, but of course why be rude to your employer? He took a load off, as directed. Keysinger took one of the Subway paper napkins from his bag, placed half a Spicy Italian on it, and extended it towards Billy, who sat slightly nervously on a second stool, unused to eating in this environment, country kitchens with center islands and stools, expanses of clean granite. Keysinger liked companionship. The morning had left him feeling somewhat irritable, and he was happy to be away from Tim Vallone and the others, whose creativity hadn't exactly overwhelmed him, but at least he wouldn't have to eat alone.

"How's the work going?" Keysinger asked.

"Another few days," Billy said. He took a bite of the sub. It tasted of his own nerves. But when he swallowed, and found something else to say, there was an aftertaste that was more reassuring. "Took an extra coat. But I think that's what you'll want."

"Whatever. My wife's department."

"Is she up here?"

"Not a chance. She grew up in Minnesota. Grew up that far north and hates the cold."

"I can understand that."

Keysinger shrugged, but not dismissively. More the shrug that was equivalent to another "whatever," so that he wouldn't have to say the word again, an elegant variation.

When two men eat together, it will happen that even when they're silent, or possibly especially if they're silent, something of a sympathetic or even symbiotic nature may develop, and it's not necessarily because they're each ignorant of what the other's thinking. "Breaking bread together," one way to say it, as if you could hear the sound of the bread breaking, and the little charm, human company, hidden in the sound. Billy found himself growing less anxious in the boss's presence, enough so that finally he asked, "What are you doing up here yourself, you don't mind my asking?"

It brought back to Keysinger the morning's unpleasant aspects, yet he couldn't find a decent reason not to answer. "Ahh, you know we've got the shoe business in town that we're trying to keep going."

"I heard that," Billy said. "I've got my brother, my dad, they all work over there, my sister-in-law … " This was out of his mouth before Billy remembered that Keysinger had mentioned "three Hutchinses" the first time they met. Billy felt there might be some demerits there, in forgetting what the boss had already told him, but Keysinger seemed to draw a blank, as if he'd clean forgotten the "three Hutchinses" at the plant, so Billy continued: "You have the chance to meet my daddy yet? Quite a character, Earl Hutchins is. If you ever get the chance … "

"Earl Hutchins … " The only reason Keysinger repeated the name, contemplatively, as if he'd be sure to keep what Billy was telling him in the forefront of memory, was that he was still trying to remember for sure whether Earl's name was on the morning's list.

Which left Billy the feeling he ought to be filling a deeper silence. "Earl, when the Bermans had the place? They had the place twenty years, the whole time Earl was in overall charge. You wanted a change of design? You went to Earl. You had trouble with the welts? You went to Earl. He did it all. You could say we're a shoe family, the Hutchinses. That's why we were grateful, believe me, when you came in."

This was flattery for sure, but Billy believed enough of it that you could say it was heartfelt flattery. "My brother Gary, he's another one. Head of the finishing."

"Oh yes." This was when Keysinger knew for sure that Earl was to be laid off – the connection to the solid finishing foreman, something he'd noted when first shown the list. He chose not to tell Billy at this particular juncture. The old question of the moment presenting itself or not.

"So the Hutchins name must be an old one around here."

"Yes, sir. I mean, sorry. Yes."

"What, there's about five families in Bealport?"

"Thereabouts. Five or six. For truth, probably, a dozen. Everybody related to everybody else, that's for sure."

"Well … I like that."

"Turns out a lot of, let's say, unusual individuals, you ask me."

"Well, that too, maybe. I wouldn't know."

"I'm saying retarded, Down Syndrome, you name it. Did I mention, I worked over at Norumbega myself four years?"

"You certainly did not."

"Three years, actually. Three and a half. Then I went out west. Felt I had to see a little more of things."

"Well that can't hurt."

"A few winters without winter. That was another thing."

"You and my wife."

"Mind my asking, Mr. Keysinger, but how's the plant doing? They going to make it over there?"

Keysinger stopped before putting out an answer. Part of this was tactical, considering that if Billy was a Hutchins, and there were Hutchinses at the plant, he didn't necessarily want his off-the-cuff remarks circulating around, especially to those who might be in position to line them up with what he'd said in reply to an altogether similar question at breakfast. "Want a Coke?" "No, but thanks." Keysinger wanted another himself, so went to the fridge. "You sure?" "Half a one. Thank you."

It was time enough for Keysinger to arrange his thoughts. "Let me ask you something, Billy. If I say something to you, is it going to get back to everybody over there, or can you keep it to yourself?"

"To myself. Absolutely, Mr. Keysinger."

"You mean that?"

"Absolutely."

"Because I feel I can trust you."

"Oh, you can."

"Then I'll tell you in two words. I'm concerned."

Keysinger fixed him with a look that Billy took as meaningful, eyebrows arched, lips pruned, as if his next words might have the force of a dart.

Billy felt to tread carefully. "About what exactly would you be concerned about, Mr. Keysinger?"

Billy was trying to train himself to say "Mr. Keysinger" when he would otherwise still have the impulse to say "sir."

"Well, we're not putting a lot of shoes in the stores. That's normal enough, I can live with that. But what concerns me … I don't feel a spark. We had a meeting this morning. You know, in a business, I'll tell you one thing I've learned. Things can get slow. You can have bad quarters. You can take bad years, even. But what you need, it's that spark, it's that thing that says, 'We're going to do something, we're going to turn something around.'"

"That's pretty bad, I guess, if you don't have that," Billy said.

"I'm not saying it's not there. I just didn't feel it today. And it concerns me," Keysinger said. To punctuate, he took the last bite of his sub, pushing into his mouth a large remainder that he otherwise might have taken in two.

What does it feel like to come upon, unexpectedly, as if you were just walking along a road somewhere and a stranger comes up to you and offers it, the one chance that for all your adult years you've been at one and the same time expecting and giving up on ever seeing? To Billy, oddly, it felt like a no-lose proposition. Danger and surprise were only a part of it, the frosting or the fizz or one of those.

Whether he knew it or not, he felt the wonder of having nothing to lose.

He swigged his Coke, approximately self-confidently, then said: "You'd be due for some changes, seems like to me. You're the businessman, you're seeing it a hundred times better, but could I tell you something, Mr. Keysinger? I do know a couple things about shoes. Not just listening to the old man for thirty years. From my time there, from when the Bermans had the place. Now they were good people, but they let the idiots run the asylum, if you know what I mean."

You can run your mouth quite a ways when everything's been stored as long as Billy had stored it. Keysinger was actually fascinated that the handyman had so many words in him. Until then, he'd seemed a quiet type. Billy kept going:

"What am I talking about? I'm talking about point A, they demoted old Earl, which, okay, I can understand that to an extent, I'm not saying he didn't have some problems with the liquor – but then the Bermans sold the place, and the new people didn't replace him! There was never another head of product development. So where were they going to get the new products from? Now under the Bermans we had a full line. We had lace-ups, we had brogues, oxfords, dress boots, cordovans, you name it. There's people there know how to make all those things, top of the line. But, oh no, the wisdom was, people are not buying the old kind of shoes. Well if they're not buying the old kind of shoes, what are you still making loafers for? Oh, that's different. Well, how's it different? They said, your penny loafer, that's a perennial. People want their penny loafer made in America. But what about brogues? What about cordovans? When I got to the plant, we were making the best cordovan shell monk straps in the country, which happens to mean, probably, all I know, the world. Why was that? To start, the Bermans bought the best cordovan, the leather itself, right from Chicago, the best tannery there was, Horvath's. You know Horvath's?"

Keysinger confessed that he didn't.

"The best tannery there was, for shell cordovan. They quit using Horvath's. Why? Well you don't need the best shell cordovan if you don't make the best shoe out of 'em. And that's just one example. It was like they didn't know the world past their own noses. I'm talking about the Ohio company, that took over. I was out in California. Even there, you could see it. Home of all the sport shoes, right? Everybody with their Nikes and Pumas. Sure, but the business guys, in the big buildings? They're making more money than ever and they want real shoes. You don't go to your million dollar job in Nikes. Or in Florsheims. You make good money, you want the best. And the best is what we stopped making. You know what that place out in Wisconsin gets for wingtips? Three hundred, four hundred dollars. We should be making five hundred dollar wingtips. We used to make wingtips. Not any more. Gear up. Go back to Horvath. Do what you do best and charge a mint because we're living in a rich man's world. That's my position. Not that anybody's asking."

"Well. I guess I was," Keysinger said.

Billy wasn't finished. He may even have felt that Keysinger was egging him on, enjoying him, clown that he was. "I don't even know anymore, have they still got the punch press to make the eyeholes? Probably rusting in some corner. Never mind, there's gotta be punch presses all over the state. The machinery's available. Somebody's just got to get it out, clean off the cobwebs. It's not like it's going-to-the-moon money. I wouldn't think so, no way. Just know where your weaknesses are. Know who's not doing the job. Be a little smart and you'd be back in business … Sorry, did I blow it?"

"You didn't blow it," Keysinger said. "Not yet."

"It didn't sound like I was trying for a job or whatnot?"

"Actually, it did."

"Oh. Uh-huh." The air started coming out of Billy, but even as Keysinger could see all the flaws and caveats, he was smiling – inwardly a lot, outwardly a hint, some would say the typical distribution of a man of business – for the fact that somebody appeared to have a spark. Keysinger had always been something of a believer in the last shall be first. Or, another, more Zen-y version that he was known to thrown around at business retreats, sometimes those that are near are far and vice versa. It just made sense, when you thought about it. It went with the world being by nature and scientific fact topsy-turvy. Meanwhile, for his part, Billy assumed he'd blown it.

"Let me ask you something, Billy. If I was going to offer you a position over at Norumbega, and it could be whatever position you wanted, but the one thing I'd insist on, you choose whichever it is where you feel you could make the biggest contribution to turning the place around, what would it be?"

Billy felt enough of a rush to feel he had to resist it, normal operating procedure for a man over thirty years old who in his personal estimate had never had a good deed go unpunished in his lifetime.

"As just hypothetical, right?"

"Right. Just hypothetical."

"I'd say, product development."

"Head of product development?"

"Whatever."

"Head of product development."

"As I believe I was suggesting, Mr. Keysinger, unless something's changed that I wouldn't know, the position's not filled. No position, no development. It's a negative situation," Billy said.

"Now, hypothetically, a second thing. If you were head of product development and I told you, whatever else you did, you had to report only to me, you'd be my eyes and ears, I'd be your sounding board and vice versa, and everybody else, you'd just have to negotiate so feelings weren't out of joint and turf wars weren't breaking out morning and night – in other words, you'd be my man, but you'd have to be a little bit careful about it – do you think you could do that? Hypothetically."

"Could take a little practice, but you know … sure. 'Course I could. I could do anything you ask."

Keysinger felt gratified, because he'd chosen to wait for the moment, and now the moment had arrived. "What about this one, hypothetically? I tell you we've got to lose some people from the workforce. I tell you we've got to lose your dad. Earl. If I told you to, would you fire him?"

"Fire Earl? I most definitely would." Billy said it without a second's hesitation, and Keysinger took note that Billy said it without a second's hesitation, as if it were a question he'd been waiting for all afternoon.

That one question, that one answer, as if Billy had solved a koan. With it, Billy Hutchins got the newly-restored position of Head of Product Development at Norumbega Footwear.

It was as much to shake up his own mind as anything that Keysinger hired Billy. It was a lark, it was a huge mistake fondly embraced. He didn't even check on Billy's past, perhaps because he suspected that if he did, he would find things that would be hard to ignore. He simply liked the guy. He liked his hungry look and his famished gush of words. And he realized, if it didn't work out, that he could just as easily fire Billy in two weeks' time. He wasn't marrying the guy. He was just looking for a spark to start a blaze.

Billy was quick to accept whatever salary Keysinger offered. It wasn't that much really. Sean and Kristen were both paid more. Gary got paid almost as much. But "Head of Product Development," that was something – even the way you got to capitalize the words. The first thing Billy thought of – for he didn't yet know that his salary exceeded Gary's, which would have been the first thing if he'd known – was that he'd have another BMW pretty soon. Maybe not a new one, but at least a Beemer, as he'd had out west.

And Earl didn't get fired. His name came off the list. Billy said he could use him.

The News

It went in all directions, so it was hard to get a grasp of it. The layoffs, the return of Billy. Mary Francis, after twenty-seven years. Charlie Russell, after nineteen years. The list. And why these, and not others? People of course were inclined to try to figure that part out. Burton was red-rimmed from trying to think about Mikey. Of course he would be at anyone's top of the list, but what Burton couldn't figure out was why they'd bother giving out the raises in the first place. You get raises, but you lose Mikey. As he'd feared right along, you gain ten percent, but you lose one hundred percent. Or at least some did. There was a feeling at the McDonald's of solidarity on the one hand, and there-but-for-the-grace-of-God on the other.

And some others took the opportunity for a little quiet score-settling and I-told-you-so. Dot Bowden from the cutting department was of the opinion, for example, that Pammy Harrelton had never cut her weight and usually left the most difficult hides for others. Dot had let these feelings of hers be previously known in private, but now she said the facts spoke for themselves, she was sorry but there you had it. There were one or two other similarly regretful confessions of the unfortunate shortcomings of the fallen, but mostly the mood was mournful, quiet, and uncertain. And who were they thinking was going to do the extra work, with ten percent of everybody gone?

Burt Miles further expressed himself that the real problem was that they were flailing around and didn't have a clue. By "they" he was of course referring to the people upstairs or the people down in Connecticut, as the case may be. Others were loathe to take issue with Burton directly, on account of his unhappiness concerning Mikey and because he was sleepless, but that didn't mean they concurred entirely. Indeed it was remarkable how much reasonableness and even sympathy for the problems of management a number of the workers maintained. They weren't just sucking up, either, as there was no one in the McDonald's worth sucking up to. It's hard to sell shoes, Peg Eaton said. It's all about price, Fox Herman said, these days it's all that mattered with people, price, price, and price. But wasn't that true of themselves included, Marge Deschamps asked. Of course it was, because themselves included didn't have the money, so what else were they supposed to do, Pete Hammond wanted to know. Dawn Smith remembered, correctly, that there'd been layoffs often enough in the past, and that when things perked up, you got hired back. It had happened to Dawn twice herself. But Dawn was perhaps too optimistic, in the view of the others. Dawn was known in general to be a little too optimistic, so that when she spoke, people tended automatically to take a discount, and to recalibrate their own opinions proportionately downward.

It was remarkable how long it took for the name of Billy Hutchins even to enter the conversation. Nobody knew what to make of it. Nobody wanted to think about it. He was a shadow in the room, waiting to pounce, to spring to life, to do some Billy Hutchins-like thing. Such things included, in the collective Bealport memory: having a considerable talent and brains that he never quite put to the best use; getting Marcia Goyne pregnant in the tenth grade; being under general suspicion of involvement in certain activities for which he was never actually charged; not getting on with his calm-natured, responsible, and generally approved-of brother; having that smile, having that sweet nature somewhere, as Alma Hutchins always swore by; and leaving town. But what was he going to do now, now that he'd come back and, most remarkably, wormed his way – excuse us, *made* his way, by who could say precisely which honorable means – into the good opinion of Rog Keysinger, savior of the town? Again, you could count on Dawn Smith to see the bright side: the company could use some new products, whoever it was, whether it was Billy or Tom Dick or Harry. Timmy Thomson could kind of see that. When you saw it in that light, he said, Madrigal was showing a lot of faith. You don't appoint a head of product development if the whole company's headed for the dumpster. But why Billy Hutchins, what were *his* qualifications, Con Bowden wanted to know. Con had never been a fan of Billy, which might have dated back to high school and girls. Pete Hammond heard he'd been working down to Keysinger's place on the Island. Burt Miles, who'd been quiet, saw a conspiracy somewhere, though he wasn't about to point any fingers yet, even if it did seem remarkable that of all the people who could be laid off, Earl Hutchins, who hadn't been sober in a year, you'd think would be at the top of any person-with-a-brain's list. Not that Burton didn't like old Earl, he loved old Earl. But were these hard times or weren't they? They ought to make up their goddamn minds.

Burton was still in that bitter mood when Charlie Russell's pickup was seen pulling into the lot. Marge Deschamps nodded in the direction of the blue Dodge Ram and the room quieted down, though it would be some seconds yet before Charlie made his appearance. By the time he arrived, if you left out the sounds behind the counter, it was mortuary quiet. Charlie had kids but they were grown. He was married to Janet, but she worked up in Bangor. It wouldn't be easy for them but it wouldn't be impossible. Like Burton Miles, Charlie had been up at night, mostly thinking about why it was himself and not some of these other ne'er-do-wells, but he had come to no conclusions. You don't want to think work's too important, especially if it's all day the same, you want to think family and fishing and hunting are important and then there's this time taken out of the middle whereby you get to pay the bills – but all that tends to be theory, once the job's gone. The foregoing was what Charlie was working out in his mind, where things tended to repeat themselves now and not make any progress. The most solid thing he could wrap around was the unemployment insurance. How many weeks was it now? Twenty-six, thirty-nine, fifty-two? It was a funny way to look at the year, to divide it up that way instead of by the seasons, but there's no question that when it has to, the mind will follow the money. He'd be calling the federal office in Bangor as soon as it opened.

"I'm going to clean out the lake, Burt. There won't be a bass left in the weeds by the time you jokers get out there." This was Charlie putting the lipstick on the pig. He was a big man with a stomach and big ears that looked sunburned even in winter and a good head of hair that wasn't gone at all. He had one coronary under his belt and some knee problems that slowed him but otherwise was hale for forty-nine. He was quick to tell people the coronary wasn't major, as he'd been out of Eastern Maine in forty-eight hours.

"Bad news." "Sorry, Charlie." "You'll be back." The things that are said, as if he were a ballplayer sent back to the minors. It wasn't that the workers of Norumbega were unfamiliar with these scenes. Though it was sometimes hard to be as convincing as once they might have been.

Charlie sat down crosswise on one of the rooted chairs. He didn't even go for a coffee.

On this occasion in particular he seemed heavier than everyone else, seemed to have a gravitational pull. The others either let him alone or made a few jokes. Charlie said to Burt how badly he felt about Mikey. Burt thanked Charlie with odd formality: "I appreciate your thoughtfulness." The bright primary colors of the McDonald's decor seemed to quiet down then, seemed to retreat from their jokey assertion of well-being, as if Ronald McDonald himself had been put to silence by the brief exchange between these two men.

People sat with Charlie until ten to eight, when they patted him and went off to the plant. A few minutes later he was still sitting there, still without a coffee.

A Dialogue Between Brothers

The following was at Gary's place, in the evening, in the garage, where Gary was pounding some damage out of the Lincoln, on the first occasion that Billy had been by in five years.

BILLY *(of the car)*: "Getting there."

GARY *(not looking up much from his workbench)*: "Guess so."

BILLY: "I'll be starting up Monday."

GARY: "Hey, that's great, Billy. All the best with that."

BILLY: "Wouldn't of believed it, huh? Few years ago, your younger brother, Head of Product Development?"

GARY: "Big responsibility, Billy. Just don't blow it."

BILLY: "You suggesting that's my nature, I blow things?"

GARY: "I'm not suggesting anything. I'm just reciting history."

BILLY: "Well thanks a big bundle, bro. Thanks a big shitpile."

GARY: "Take it easy."

BILLY: "I'm takin' it very easy. You think I don't know my responsibility? You know how hard I had to work just to keep old Earl on?"

GARY: "He was on the list?"

BILLY: "Damn fucking straight he was on the list."

GARY: "Well … okay."

BILLY: "That's all you can say, is okay? I put my skinny ass on the line. I said I'd watch over him."

GARY: "I thought I'd been watching him pretty good myself. Guess you wouldn't know, not having been around."

BILLY: "If that's a sarcastic tone, it wouldn't be necessary."

GARY: "No sarcastic tone. Just facts."

BILLY: "Well thanks a lot then. Good to see you."

GARY: "Thanks for stopping by." *(as Billy starts for the garage door)* "If you're Earl's big protector now, you can stop by Durfee's, see if he's in there. That's what I've been doing. You take him home if he's in there."

BILLY: "Always appreciate your advice, big brother."

When Billy was gone, Gary pounded harder on the strip of bumper he'd been pounding out. Realizing it was his knee-jerk reaction and that he was going to do the bumper no good, he gave it up for the night and went to the house to watch some television. Martha handed him the channel changer. She asked how it was to see Billy and did he say much about any of what was going on. Gary shrugged. All he could think was that Billy didn't know a dime's worth about shoes, or if you were going to be generous about it, maybe he knew a couple things, but not in comparison to Gary himself. But since he'd already expressed that opinion to Martha as many as three times in the week, he chose to stay quiet and watch a show about men off the Philippines hunting for sunken treasure. The fish swimming around, the hint of a Manila galleon in watery outline, the predictable appearance of a shark or two. On these programs, there was always a shark or two.

Gary hoped he would dream about the galleon, the ghost ship, everything about it fallen off and encrusted, a sweet dream, him swimming in the murky water towards it, and getting there or not but probably not, which would be even better, to be forever swimming towards the dream that he was also in, and he would not wake up at four thinking about Billy.

The Thought

When he woke up, the clock accused him of it being four-seventeen. He couldn't remember any dream. The back of his neck sweated into the pillow. He held still and took deep breaths because sometimes deep breaths put him back to sleep. Martha was not budging beside him. His thought was of the high card he would never play. Was he or wasn't he, that was one way to think of it. Was he or wasn't he one of only three people – the others being the Bermans who were now living in Naples, Florida – who knew why Billy left working for Norumbega Footwear in the first place? More generally, Gary felt the question to be about himself: was he or wasn't he?

Winter Soldiers

Burton and Bev were concerned again about Mikey. There were periods, actually, when they were not too concerned, when life went along and their son was who he was, for whom they had no more or better or sincerer words to put to than his name. But the layoff hit Mikey hard. The biggest problem was that he had nothing to do all day. Or anyway this was as Burt and Bev understood it, who only went as deep into a problem as their minds could bear without aching. This approach was called common sense. But it didn't keep Bev from voicing the additional complaint that the health plan the company offered, and at considerable expense to the employees, didn't cover mental situations. Burt would point out to her that because Mikey was laid off, and because he was past the age to be covered on their own benefits, it made no difference if Norumbega offered mental health coverage or not, but this only enflamed her grievance. They lay a boy like Mikey off, then give him no tools to cope. With his parents out of the house, Mikey retreated to the three year old Dell downstairs. It's perhaps some commentary on the nature of the digital world that it was Mikey's greatest field of competence, if you chose to measure competence by the percentage at which he could perform and understand a given activity relative to most other people. It was for this reason, mainly, that for some years his parents had been "liberal" in terms of seldom chasing Mikey off the computer. It was a learning device, they would tell people, and probably it was. It was also, in the new millennium, the way most of Bealport connected to the wider world. A godsend to the small towns, you heard that all the time. Mikey spent his days playing the games, which were mostly shooting games. He found it an advantage that he knew how to shoot a real gun. An uncertain pride, as well. It occurred to him that about this one thing he might know more than most. He manned fighter planes, drones, spacecraft, time warp machines, thought projection destroyers, and transformers with knives, claws, and grenade launchers for hands. None of these assuaged his hurt, which went into the games and disappeared a little while only to come out of it with its dreary watery simulacrum unscathed. He could not understand how the best box-putter-together in Bealport could be laid off. He had been told many times that he was the best box-putter-together. His father had even told him. Who would put the boxes together now? He asked his father, who never had a good answer, because he didn't care to say that it was he himself who was now doing at least Mikey's share of it. Or that it had been a make-work job for Mikey for years, because the Bermans had been kindly people, and the subsequent folks from American Shoe had never quite caught on to what had been set up during the Bermans' time. When his hurt came back to him, Mikey felt very angry. Who were these people who did this? The new people, everybody said, but who was new and who was not? It seemed like the same people, except they hated him now, so he hated them back. It was only fair. You kill one of me, I kill two of you. The way to score high, the way to be a game winner. And two, shmoo. Mikey didn't know what a shmoo was. It was more like ten or a hundred. You could be a game winner if you shmooed that many. Bev began talking to Burt about getting Mikey a therapist on their own. It would be a stretch, but what else could they do? When he was in school, Mikey always had a therapist. The last few years, it was like his job had become his therapist, and Mikey had thrived.

It was enough of a stretch of the budget to hire a therapist that Burton consulted his fellow Winter Soldiers on the subject, as to whether they had had similar experience and what they thought. *Wsmuncie6* commented, somewhat predictably, Burton felt, that therapists were a New World Order invention. *Wsstormboy* went further, having studied the UNESCO charter, which showed that it was the United Nations that was the number one promoter of psychotherapy in the entire world, and that eventually, if it wasn't stopped, there would be billions – not millions, but billions – of people worldwide under "care." *Wswesternmass19* opined that this could be the best possible result, let them poison the whole rest of the world, it would be another case of competitive advantage for those Americans who would be left as holdouts. *Wsholton* seconded that: the way the world was going, we could use every advantage we could get, and if they were stupid enough to go poison themselves, so be it. That would be a good one, *wswatchtower* gloated, poison themselves with an American invention, which would serve them only right, always shitting on America. *Wsgeorgewashingtonbridge* was quick to correct *wswatchtower* on the origins of therapy, saying it was Freud who was an Israeli by the way who invented it. *Wsfrankr* chided the rest for having strayed totally from the request of *wsbealport1* for advice re what he should be doing in his situation. *Wslancaster3* apologized to *wsbealport1* for the diversion and suggested that the best would be to get the damn job back from the UN-loving types who took it away from him, but if that wasn't in the cards which it probably wasn't, then the next best thing would be to boycott the whole company, if every Winter Soldier took it upon himself or herself to boycott, then maybe the situation could still be turned around, as one thing you could say about these cosmopolitan international banker types is the bottom line is their one god. *Wsbealport1* thanked *wslancaster3* for the suggestion, but said he had doubts a boycott would be effective, because how many Winter Soldiers bought Norumbega shoes to start with?

The Prodigal

For his first official act, or the first anyway that he would imagine and project symbolically, the new Head of Product Development went out to Chicago and bought shell cordovan from Horvath's. He felt it was important to do this in person and to show that he knew one hide from another. In the evening he went to a nearby bar and met a girl from Sioux City whom sometime around three in the a.m. he showed, in his personal opinion, a very good time. This perk, however self-achieved, made up somewhat for having to fly coach.

Around the plant, he was everywhere. Every department received his visit once, sometimes twice, an hour. Yet he managed not to be too much of a jerk about it. This was of course what Keysinger had requested of him. Billy was a quick study. In fact he went to the little Bealport library, where he hadn't been twice in his life, and got out tapes on management. He listened in the car and watched at home, which he could do because he had quickly acquired both car and home, having taken an apartment over Ralphie's on Main Street and a lease on a well-aged starter BMW off a corner car lot in Bangor. The modest nature of these acquisitions reflected the fact that Billy had decided to spend less than he was taking in. What had come over the boy?

As Billy unpacked it to himself, this was a chance that who knew how often it came along or probably never so why fuck around with it. If this was a conventional sentiment, he didn't seem to care or notice. When he went into one of the departments and asked Con, or Martha, or Burt, or whoever, how this or that was going or whether they had any suggestions for the new line of cordovan monk straps, he didn't remind them that the new line was all his idea, or what his title was by inference or otherwise, nor did he suggest they had to do it his way or the cliché about the highway. He was all ears, which was pretty funny, considering that Billy had often been kidded, from the first year he went to school, for his good-sized ears. With Gary, he was quieter, but not impolite. "Howdy bro," "need anything?" That sort of durable approach, as if dealing with a respected equal from whom most of all he wanted no trouble. Gary responded in kind, so that they were like two animals of different species and approximately equal capabilities examining each other from an understood distance.

It was only with Earl that Billy was otherwise. In one of the library books, a management guru with a nautical background had declared that he'd rather have a fighting spirit in his crew than everybody happily complacent and harmonious but destined for the lifeboats. This was the approach Billy took to his father, whose job he had saved after all, whose praises he had sung to the boss. Billy had always been afraid of his father, but now the fear was of a different cast – he was afraid his father would embarrass him. Did Earl really know as much about shoes as Billy had claimed? From the first day that he had to depend on him, Billy hated the legends of Earl. They were the past excusing the future, and Billy was all about the future now. He knew where Earl stashed liquor at the camp and regularly cleaned those places out. He massaged Jim Terry at Durfee's to cut Earl off after two beers. He called Earl each morning at six forty-five. You could say, in one sense, he had taken what Gary said to him to heart. Either that or he was showing Gary how it was done. And that was only the half of it. The other half was seeing what Earl actually knew, harnessing what was left of his spirit. He convened something like a tutorial with Earl at the plant each morning before the actual workday. It consisted, often enough, of Billy detailing to Earl some new idea he had and Earl telling him how to do it and Billy telling Earl they couldn't do it quite like that for various reasons, among them that it didn't make any sense, and Earl telling his son to fuck off then and not bother him if he wasn't going to listen, and Billy finally listening with one ear and using what he could of it. One thing Earl remembered perfectly well was how to work with the shell cordovan. Earl, who considered himself an artist manqué, though he may have lacked the portfolio or the phrase, still had the artist's affinity for the very best materials. They inspired and sharpened him up. He sat at his bench a little straighter when he had a stack of first class leather in front of him, as if the very smell of it sobered him up. In a month, Norumbega was producing as fine a pair of monk straps as it ever had. They were sleek, they held the foot, they gave where they had to, you could walk a hundred miles in them and not even know they were on your feet. And, as Billy noted, you could get top dollar for them.

So it was something of a productive partnership, the prodigal son and the dissolute father. Earl didn't know what to make of Billy. He certainly didn't trust his success. He felt that of course the kid had always had it in him, he loved Billy with the wild swings of love that certain kinds of fathers have, the repressed giving way to the sentimental, the sentimental savagely beaten back, but he kept waiting for him to fuck it up. Nothing personal necessarily about it, just genetics: it didn't quite make sense to Earl for the Hutchinses to have made such a comeback. As for the drink, he could live with it or without it, which was what he had always claimed, that he was never an alcoholic but only bored. A man must have pleasures in his life but now he had a new one. Not that Billy didn't piss him off on a daily basis. The little fucking know-it-all, the insinuations, the way he didn't even seem to notice that Earl noticed the insinuations. But, to put it mildly, what were you going to do? Earl had taken to bragging about Billy all the time, over at Durfee's, in the Hannaford, at the McDonald's. There wasn't a chance of anyone in Bealport being unaware that Billy was Earl Hutchins' son, and that his son was seeking his father's advice on many significant aspects of what was going on over there at the plant.

A dialogue between Billy and Earl:

BILLY *(on the occasion of Earl missing their morning meeting and showing up half-plastered at eleven)*: You know I could fire your ass so fast? I could kick your ass so far out of here you'd never find your way back. You're on probation, Earl."

EARL: "The fuck pussy talk is that? Threatening me? Threatening your dad? Just get it over with then. Whole place run by pussies. Think I give a dick's piss?"

BILLY: "You will. You will."

EARL *(mocking)*: "I will. I will."

BILLY: "Pathetic old rummy."

EARL: "Least I'm not other certain things I could name."

BILLY: "You name whatever you want, Earl. I got work to do."

EARL: "Me too."

BILLY: "Well aren't we glad to see you remembered."

EARL: "If I could just get a little peace and quiet here."

BILLY: "Have a good day then."

EARL: "You too, son."

BILLY: "You too, Earl … Stick of Doublemint?"

EARL: "I'd be honored."

BILLY "You're still on probation."

Anger, then, like the sea, crests, troughs, crests, and with comic interludes where the sea laughs at itself, as if to suggest a more permanent state of affairs than could ever be. By April the plant was producing monk straps in a grainy cowhide as well as cordovan, Blucher wingtips, Balmoral wingtips, a wingtip moccasin, the traditional Norumbega loafer, and a line of white bucks for summer.

A Warmer Climate

There was still dirty snow in the corners of Bealport when Rog Key-singer arrived in Santa Fe, New Mexico for a conference organized by the American Institute for Leadership on the topic "Everything You Wanted to Know But Were Afraid to Ask About The Century Ahead." C.E.O.s, C.F.O.s, C.O.O.s, consultants, gurus, junior comers, the odd politician, and some individuals whose distinction was being plain rich gathered under sunny skies at a faux-adobe palatial venue just outside town. The temperature was in the pleasant sixties. Key-singer had prepared a paper on "The Love It or Leave It Syndrome." By this title he intended to challenge the assumption that globaliza-tion was an either-or proposition. Of course it was inevitable that there would be winners and losers, because there were always winners and losers. You couldn't name a human process where that wasn't the case. Moreover you might not want it otherwise, winning and losing being part of the game of life, a part that made it highly interesting, though of course the losers might dispute that. Keysinger was good natured about it all. He paid a dollop of lip service, more skeptical than not, to the so-called Walmart Syndrome, according to which workers may have been getting the shaft wage-wise and job-security-wise, but had access to a world of cheap goods they'd never had access to before. Two-hundred-dollar flat-screen T.V.s with high-def and hundreds of megahertz and many other wonderful things? Hah! The worldwide web, networking, community, shopping, porn so abun-dant you couldn't look at it all if you lived a thousand lifetimes? Hah, to all that as well. There came a point where he made mention of a little experiment he was trying with a shoe factory in Maine. He didn't dwell on it, but he mentioned it, then moved on to the pith of his argument, for which the shoe factory could be considered a kind of foreshadowing: the country was devaluing what it still had. It devalued its education, by all but pleading with students to take an interest in it, rather than presenting it as something hard, rare, desirable. It devalued its culture, by suggesting it scarcely existed except in little balkanized patches, this oppressed group or that one. It even devalued the bond with its own people, by making citizenship little harder to obtain than a driver's license. The country was awash in all kinds of jingoism, sentimentality, and cheap billboard pride in itself, but where was the right kind of pride, sober, modest, soft-spoken, a little bit austere? There ought to be room in the world both for billions of its poor to do better and for the country to continue to do well. Protectionism of the spirit, that was the phrase he finally got to. He had cadged it off a commencement speech he previously delivered at a small upstate New York college.

A decent ripple of applause greeted Keysinger's conclusion, in intensity and duration slightly exceeding what seemed the conference average. A few amens or words to that effect swam in the undertow. He had spent the hours in the Lear from Connecticut honing the speech, like a stand-up comic after a performance of new material rigorously reviewing what got laughs and what didn't, and when he was done, as a kind of bonus he granted himself for his conscientiousness, he believed every word of it. So fuck 'em if they couldn't, so to speak, take a joke, if they thought of him as no more than "above average." Despite his successes in various endeavors, Keysinger took his role in the world to be someone who was not quite believed. In the question period, a woman asked whether he was being critical of Walmart. She was a woman in her forties with a dark wave of hair and Mediterranean eyebrows. Keysinger went a long way around to say that he wasn't sure whether he was or he wasn't. Afterwards she came up to him with more questions and they continued to debate. The debate went on awhile, and flowed out of the conference room, until it became impossible to tell whose side which one was on, or if there were sides at all. At this point, it became more interesting.

The Ministry

The Reverend John Quigley was aware of currents of opinion in Bealport which held that he was not much interested in God. He took few pains to dispel these rumors, if that's what they were, because he was not sure if they were true or false. He believed that some principle akin to Heisenberg's in physics was at play with belief, in that the very act of asking if it were true or not effected some change in the answer, so that you might be left feeling closer but still not sure, surety itself becoming a leaping, mocking thing. He feared that he had come to God too young. To believe in God when you were six because it was what you were told; to believe in God when you were nine because it only made sense; to believe in God at fifteen because otherwise the pain of the world would be unbearable. Too much time was left for doubt. Would it not have been better for belief to come late, when there was less time to reverse the outcome, the way certain sports teams manage to rally as the clock winds down or armies to counterattack just before both sides are exhausted? Then, too, he felt that there might be a balance of payments issue. He had spent, in aggregate, and give or take, depending what you cared to count, twelve years of his life in prayer. Should not those years then be followed by twelve years doing the Lord's work in the world? God would not forget that he had prayed. God would want him to *do* something now. This was conjecture on Quigley's part, but everything was conjecture. He was still a young man, with a Bible in one hand and Karl Marx in the other.

Though had the latter in Quigley's incomprehension and doubt become one more guilty pleasure, like the charades at the Shady Lady? His *Capital* had arrived at the church, after all, in plain

Amazon brown, the way smutty materials used to go through the mails. One more febrile try at being in the world but not of it, but how else know what the world needed? The old argument, that even Quigley could see how the Devil might make. You could even say he was a glutton for mystification, sitting up in his bed the nights when "Marylou" worked, scribbling rows of question marks until it was too embarrassing to scribble any more of them in the margins, all so that he could understand if it was a matter of scientific inevitability that his congregants were getting screwed.

For this was what he felt was happening. At the next setback, would there not be more layoffs? Quigley felt it was a question not of if but of when, and then, more urgently, came the question of what to do about it. His congregants would have understood neither a Bible thumper nor a bomb thrower. Nor would Quigley himself. He simply wanted a little justice to be done, a little of God's work making its way through the world and down to this tiny bunch of powerless, ill-equipped, antiquated people who for better or worse for two and a half years had been his to fuss and think about. And did he love them, as he was commanded to? Leave that for another day. When the end of April came and those who'd been laid off were not recalled, the Reverend Quigley called a meeting.

He called it for a Wednesday evening, in hopes that his fifty or a hundred regulars would be augmented by some less spiritually oriented citizens. Or, no, scratch that ironic construction. By persons who didn't go to church, but who for all the Reverend Quigley knew might be secret yogis, Buddhists, Zoroastrians, firewalkers. He put signs up on the lampposts and in Ralphie's Pizza and a notice in the paper, gave the meeting a name, NEXT TIME LET'S BE PREPARED, and wound up with a crowd that filled the pews. It astonished and heartened him, really. People cared about the plant. Of course a cynic might say it was all they had.

It was like Christmas Eve, without the singing or the snowy cheeks. Martha Hutchins was there and the rest of the crew of sewers. The whole cutting department was there. All those who'd been laid off were there, with the one exception of Mikey Miles, whom Burton thought best not to bring, for the possibility that he'd make a fuss or grow still more despondent. At home they were still trying to get his mind off the layoff. Among other notable no-shows was Gary Hutchins, who believed it was a waste of time and mistrusted the pastor for what he imagined might be union organizing. Gary was not against union organizing in principle, but considered it unsuited to the local conditions and population, which didn't need any out-of-state mafias telling it what to do and not do, not to mention the union dues that would probably be going to somebody's trip to Cancun.

Quigley thought long and hard over the question whether to wear the collar that night, like a kid in front of the mirror with it on then with it off, a touch of authority or the common touch. In the end he went for both. Jeans and the collar, something for everybody, God and the people. Not to say his fashion sense, his place in the world. Were these quiet people in front of him admiring that very fashion sense? He did not make the mistake of interpreting their quiet as mildness or passivity. He simply didn't know what it was, or which way it might go. Reaching back for something he'd read somewhere, gripping the lectern with both hands as if he might at any moment have to raise it up to fend off an attack, he imagined the people of Bealport in front of him having a negative capability. And then he began by saying "Good morning." It was a mistake but it broke the ice. His smile was embarrassed and thin. "Sorry. I thought it was Sunday morning. Good *evening*."

There was a surprisingly hearty "Good evening" in response. Some of the newcomers must have known the drill from somewhere or sometime. Quigley wondered if it was the same in A.A. as in the church, but never mind. The first thing he wanted to share with the community, once the time of day was straightened out, was that he wasn't some shill for a union, as he'd heard a few folks in the village speculating on. He then moved to the matters at hand, the layoffs, the prospects, the next time. He didn't really get many ears pricked up until he came to his "original" idea for the evening, which he confessed people were going to find unusual, but these were not usual times. He pushed his dated wire rims back up his long aquiline nose, down which they had slid on the surface of his sweat, and declared, "I've heard the boss over there likes the phrase, 'All for one and one for all.' Well, you know something? I do believe he's right. What about, the next time there's layoffs, instead of just losing people, we go over there to Mister Vallone, and suggest everybody in the plant works however many fewer hours, two or three, whatever's necessary and fair, in exchange for no layoffs?"

When Quigley heard his own words, aloud for the first time, they reeked of helplessness and well-meaningness. He was even ashamed of them, as if he were just trying to put his two cents in, and should have done better to keep quiet if he couldn't think of anything more singular or likely. He especially wondered why he had to put in the word "fair." It could sound like a concession. Who cared if their sacrifice was fair, so long as for once his people got something? He also questioned why he hadn't called Vallone by his first name.

The hundred and fifty faces in front of him looked especially expressionless when he was done. Until Burton Miles stood up, after what might have been either due deliberation or a dramatic pause for effect, and said he'd heard something like this was being done in Germany, and they've been doing all right over there. Carl Esposito heard of a situation similar at a stove assembly plant his cousin worked at down in Massachusetts. Peg Eaton wanted to know why they were only looking to the future, why not go back and offer the same arrangement right now, try and get Mary Francis and Carl himself and Charlie and Dot and so forth back on the job.

The small miracle to John Quigley was that no one spoke against his idea, nor Peg's amendment to it. This was a village where you could find someone to speak against anything, where the typical annual town meeting lasted to two or three in the a.m. because of arguments about whether the shrubs in front of the post office should be cut back a foot or a foot and a half. Yet no one was telling Quigley he was full of it. What was wrong here? Could it be he actually had a good idea, or were they so cowed and desperate they would listen to anything? Cautiously, he reminded everyone that in the event such a plan actually went through, each one of them would find himself or herself with some amount of a cut in take home pay, at least in the short or medium term before or until the economic conditions improved, definitions of which would have to be set out in the plan so that the company couldn't cry poor forever. Dottie Bowden did ask what that cut in pay might amount to. Quigley admitted he didn't know, but imagined it might be in the vicinity of ten percent, as it had been ten percent of the workers who were let go. Burton Miles, an immediate champion of the plan, as it promised to help Mikey, volunteered that perhaps the cuts would be somewhat less, if the average wage of those laid off was somewhat lower than of the workforce as a whole.

Quigley then made a somewhat impassioned speech about the values of community and sticking together. It sounded unnecessary in his own ears, a politician's speech, a phony, but when he called for a voice vote, on the question whether a delegation from the assembled should go to the Norumbega management with their proposal, yays outnumbered nays by in the neighborhood of four to one. And in the strength and timbre of the yays, Quigley sensed he heard not desperation but something more unlikely, something tempered. Further details, of strategy, of delegates, of timing, were then opened for discussion, and some of the town's traditional feistiness then came into play, so that the meeting lasted another hour and a half. Much of the debate centered on whether Dot Weller should be one of the delegates, the problem being that Dot volunteered herself, and after all was one of those laid off, but was viewed by many as rather stupid, which they didn't care to say to her face. Marge Deschamps finally reminded Dot that with her big, kind heart she had a tendency to get over-emotional and burst into floods of tears at, let's be honest, some moments that had not always been appropriate, a few of which Marge then detailed, and besides and for good measure the committee already had seven members and, for reasons not entirely articulable, eight felt like one too many.

Tim Vallone agreed to the meeting. Reverend Quigley and some of the rest were heartened, as if they'd won an opening skirmish. Extra folding chairs were brought into the Norumbega boardroom, which had been getting more use in the past four months than it had in years. Representing the company were Vallone, Mark Brine, and Sean Byrick. Vallone said he was all ears. Quigley, Burt Miles, and Peg Eaton then spoke, laying out their plan for shared sacrifice, putting in all the caveats, for instance that a vote of all the employees would be required, with at least an eighty percent approval before anything might be done. To personalize matters, Burton painted a pathetic, touching picture of what the loss of a job can do to a son. He couldn't have done better if he'd been on one of those old shows where the more pathetic a story you tell, the more contributions roll in. When their presentations were over, Vallone thanked them. He appreciated their sincerity, their effort, and their interest. He would check with the legal beagles to be sure, but he was confident there were numerous insuperable legal obstacles to what was proposed. The finance officer, Brine, then similarly expressed his appreciation for the group's initiative, but unfortunately – and oh how the Reverend Quigley would come to fear and loathe that word "unfortunately," which in contexts such as these was the verbal equivalent of a death knell – he felt compelled to tell them that the savings under their proposal would be not what they thought, that the layoffs were designed, like all unfortunate but necessary actions, for maximum tactical impact, and that it was more than a question of dollars and cents, though dollars and cents – and here he grinned either sheepishly or slyly, it was hard to tell – were always a factor. Sean Byrick was more direct than the others. He was a plain-talking Bealport boy, after all, and his friends and neighbors would want the facts: Norumbega had had to do a little cleaning house. The people who were gone needed to be gone. Without naming names, for instance, or casting any aspersions, you can't run a company like a welfare office. Or a disability clinic, for that matter, he added, as if afraid by not naming names he'd pulled too far back from his point. Maybe once upon a time you could get away with overstaffing and goodwill appointments, but not anymore.

When it was over and they had gotten nowhere, the delegates got up and left without a word. As Sean pointed out, they were plain-spoken people, and thank-yous for agreeing to the meeting or hearing their case didn't fit in their mouths.

At Rog Keysinger's specific instruction, Billy Hutchins had been kept away. His name was never mentioned. This was to preserve, in a sense, his protective coloration, his ability to swim in the waters unscathed. Keysinger realized he would be too easy a figure to hate. And hatred, discord, animosity, were still the enemies of Keysinger's conception of success, at least as it applied to an old shoe factory on the coast of Maine. Why bother with it at all if it was going to give him an ulcer? John Quigley in a bitter mood went home and got his *Capital* down from its shelf, but he read a few pages – pages six hundred seventy-two through six hundred seventy-five, to be precise – and didn't understand it any better this time than all the times before. There is no solace, he thought, nor forgetting, when you've let people down.

The Shopper

When it came to clothes, Gary never bought anything for himself other than work gloves, so that it was up to Martha to fill in the rest of his needs. Also to determine those needs, in this case for underpants. On his own, Gary would wear underpants that were all holes from so many washings or that would fall to his knees, on account of the elastic being stretched, if they weren't held mostly in place by pants and a belt on top of them. With respect to Gary, Martha sometimes thought of the old polite society saw about never wearing dirty underwear because you never knew if it was the day you would die. The horror, really, of dying on the street in underwear that told a tale. Not that Martha was from the gentry, but there had always been certain aspirations in her line, and attitudes, ideas, acquired somewhere and passed along. They were respectable people, the Pierces, no matter where they worked or how much they made. And, for example, they had always felt themselves a little above the Hutchinses, on account of the number of ministers, particularly in the nineteenth century, in the family tree. Martha kept a portrait of one, the Reverend Thomas Pierce, in a downstairs closet. She didn't hang it on a wall for everyday viewing because it had been in her parents' house and, with its cold lacquer finish that seemed to shine in the dark giving an aura of almost prophetic certitude and extra-sensory vision to the Reverend's expression of consternation, it reminded her too much of her mother's early death from cancer. The Reverend had seen the future and it gave him an upset stomach – that's how Martha, in her lighter moods, tried to dismiss its lingering impression.

Martha was a huge fan of the Bangor Target store, though she was made uncomfortable by that phony French slanging of the name that everybody, and particularly Dawn Smith and Ging Richards, were putting out there as though it was so cute and clever. Martha took it to be French-Canadian, anyway. Anything French heard or seen in Bealport she assumed to be *quebecois*, as in Marge Deschamps' long-departed, good-for-nothing husband, leaving her with two kids and one salary and a name not everyone bothered to correctly pronounce. The Target was Martha's emblem of prosperity in a way, with its clean aisles and general brightness and logo that was so excellent you could spot it from an interstate and without a word being read or spoken know immediately you were close to something familiar. You wouldn't want to get Martha Hutchins started on the superiority of the Target to the Walmart's. As long as she and Gary had their paychecks, she would be willing to spend the few pennies more, for the way the Target could almost equalize you with a rich person, on account of its general overall quality but also the designer brands that you could see in magazines, as for instance those Italian coffee pots that she still wouldn't pay the money for but that looked like they came from a movie with suave Italians drinking from little cups. Martha sometimes imagined they could use her in an ad, for a candid interview. They would approach her in the store with all their camera equipment and cords and what have you and she would only tell the truth, but with such total one hundred percent conviction that they would put her on the TV, which would go to show a certain number of persons in Bealport, but would mostly just be fun. Martha was not a resentful person, not to any extent. But what about the underpants? There was so much to look at, and so many places for her mind to wander to, that she almost forgot. It was a Saturday morning, an expedition, Gary at home in the garage.

When she finally got to the men's underpants, Martha made her decision quickly. Forget the skinny ones, the Calvin Kleins, the sexy ones, forget the jockeys or whatever they call those that are tight on a man's situation. She bought the jockeys once, Gary consented to wear them exactly one day, then she had to throw the whole three-pack out, as of course you couldn't return the two unworn pairs once the overall package was opened. She found the boxers, regular cut, assorted colors and patterns, sixty-five percent cotton, but then had to decide between the extra-large and the extra-extra-large. The fact was that Gary was squarely between these two, in terms of waist, so that the extra-large might hug a bit, but the extra-extra-large might droop. Hoping for the best, which was that Gary lose ten pounds, she narrowed her shopping to the extra-large. It was then a question simply of colors and patterns and which three-pack had the better combination, which was actually a question you could spend quite a lot of time with, as no three-pack on the extra-large rack was identical to any of the others. Occasionally in the past Martha had spent such time, when she was less familiar with the merchandise and less confirmed in Gary's taste, but today she confined herself to making sure none of the underpants had anything too cute on them, like jack-in-the-boxes or mice blowing musical instruments, and when she found a pack with the combination where one was plain blue, the second was blue and light green alternating stripes, and the third was red with checkered flags that must have had to do with auto racing, she dumped them in her cart and continued on, roaming the store, all the various departments, to see what was new, winding up finally at the checkout with nothing more in her basket than the underpants. You could say it was a case of the destination being less important than the journey, or of the destination giving Martha the gift of the journey. In high school she had read a poem that said something like that, about a much longer journey, of course.

In the parking lot, her mood dampened. The sun had broken through and was glaring. Suddenly she couldn't decide how she would spend the rest of her day. Gary would be in the garage. Jerome was off somewhere. She couldn't decide if she was hungry or if she should stop for lunch. She couldn't remember if there was anything they needed from the Hannaford, to require a stop there. She had an urge to go back in the store, just to be inside it. Then for some reason she remembered something the owner of the plant, Mr. Keysinger, Mr. Roger Keysinger, had said, when he came into the McDonald's and they were all there and Burt had asked him how they were doing. "We're getting there." That was what he'd said, "We're getting there." The next day, there'd been the announcement of layoffs. But, now that she thought of it, it wasn't a lie, was it? Mr. Keysinger hadn't told a lie at all. "We're getting there" could mean anything. How close were they to getting there? It didn't say, now, did it? They could have been getting there but still be very far away. They could have only gone forward an inch. Or it could have been the only reason they were getting there or getting anywhere was they were laying off some people. There were a dozen ways you could interpret it, now that she looked back and thought about it. Martha felt vulnerable, as if she could be walking in the Target parking lot and a car could hit her because she hadn't been looking.

Berserk

There is always a logic. In anything you can name, as soon as there is a thought, there is a logic. In the situation of Mikey Miles, the logic was this: that until the new boy came, everybody liked him; that after the new boy came, he was fired; that everybody still liked him, so it must be the new boy. Or sometimes the logic was this: that he was the best box-putter-together; that the boxes needed putting together; that if they fired the best box-putter-together and there were still boxes to put together, it must be a mistake; that if it was a mistake, it had to be fixed. Or sometimes it was this: that the new boy was named Billy; that if the new boy was named Billy and he was fired because of the new boy, then the one to hate was Billy. Or sometimes this: that if shmoo was two and you were shmoo, then shmoo you and you too. Or sometimes: that the new boy Billy must be the shmoo, because no one else was two. Or: that everything was good; that everything became bad; that if everything was bad now, then he, Mikey, must be bad now too.

It was not that Mikey was short of thoughts. It was that they went around so fast that it was hard for him to catch them, or he only caught pieces. He was not fast enough. It was like catching butterflies in your hand. Mikey loved butterflies. If you caught one, they became your friend and you could look at them forever. Mikey felt this must be true, even if he'd never caught one, even if he'd only seen them fly around and land on things and escape when he put out his hand.

As for Miss Phelan, whom he'd been seeing twice a week now, she had her ways, she had her days. Why was her hair red and what did she say? Her questions were like water, flowing back and forth. Whose side was she on? He saw her twice a week and all the while the boxes were not being put together. And did anything change, was the best box-putter-together brought back to make things right? Some games you win, some games you lose. His father taught him that. But was this a game? Is that what Miss Phelan thought, when the boxes were not put together? Of course they were put together, she said. Who did she think was doing it?

This, you could say, was what he was up against. "This," like a swarm, like a cloud of bees, that were so many that you couldn't see through them, and Mikey, if he could, would put his head down and run at them. He tried it once, putting horns on his head with his fingers sticking up and running wild and whooping till his mother called him in.

But what did she expect him to do with a cloud of bees? It was the same with the games he played. They told you to do one thing, and when you did it, they told you another. You could never catch up. You could only play. So he played. They should have given him a star. When they gave him a star, they should have given him more. This was logic, too.

He was very, very angry with Miss Phelan with her red hair but he was even very, very angrier with the new boy Billy, the No Box Putter Together. Miss Phelan was nice even if he was very, very angry with her but the new boy was not nice. Miss Phelan had nothing to do with the boxes except what she said that did not change anything, but she would be safe because what if he loved her, which he did, and her red hair too. But the new boy Billy who was not nice would not be very, very safe. Don't shmoo her, shmoo him. This was his conclusion. This was logic, too.

Use your words, Mikey. What words? This was logic, shmoo.

On the 30th of April, Mikey had his bike all ready. He put oil on the chain so it was nice. He had the thirty-aught-six on the handlebars. He had a bullet in the chamber, which was a magic bullet, which was why it was only one. It was crazy. You couldn't plan it. It wasn't like shooting a bear. What else was he supposed to do? He did everything else. What his father said, what his mother said, what

Miss Phelan said, what the games said, what the butterfly said, he did it all. And still the shmoo was you.

He rode his bicycle to the gate of the plant with the thirty-aught-six on the handlebars. There was no one to notice or say. It was a little after ten in the morning and it was just beginning to rain, a light sprinkle coming down. If Mikey had any thoughts, they were not to be shared with himself. There was a gate before you got to the parking lot. From the parking lot you got to the plant. Bob Headley was the man at the gate. Bob had been the guard there twenty-four years. He saw Mikey and he saw the thirty-aught-six.

"Hey Mikey, what are you doing here?" Bob said.

"Nothing," Mikey said.

"What are you doing with that big gun?" Bob said. "Not going hunting today, are you, Mikey?"

"No," Mikey said. And, "Nothing," he added, because he wanted to answer the first question too.

Bob thought he saw a particular dullness in Mikey's eyes, as if he'd slept either too little or too much. It wasn't normal, thought Bob, who could remember the many times when those same eyes sparkled, and the way that people would say that it was easy to make Mikey happy.

"You want to see your dad?" Bob asked.

"No," Mikey said.

But Bob thought it best to call Burton anyway, so he picked up his phone. It was an old dial system that took some seconds for the extensions to go through.

Mikey had been in situations like this, where he could see things were going badly. So he did what he always did in situations where the hero confronts danger or has one chance in a thousand to save a girl on a world far away and be given all the stars there were, which was to lift his weapon in his arms. He got down from his bike.

"Mikey, settle down, okay?" Bob said, and laid the phone aside.

Then he took hold of his own gun, which he'd not drawn in twenty-four years.

Mikey saw the danger to his plans. He wished now that he had more than one magic bullet. He fumbled with his free hand in his pocket to see if he had. "The new boy," he said, and something that sounded like "the zoo." As he fumbled, Bob came out of the guard box, with the plan to take the barrel of the thirty-aught-six and turn it aside and tell Mikey to go on home until his father got there.

Mikey took the empty hand from his pocket and used it to raise the rifle at Bob Headley, who feared for his life and shot him. It was only one bullet, so it must have been a magic one. Burton Miles picked up the phone in the shipping department just in time to hear the shot through the receiver.

The Solace

John Quigley had put on his ministerial finest to see the troubled woman, who presented herself with covered hair and dressed in black. She said to him, "Reverend, I'm so grateful to you for seeing me." "Like they say, it's what I'm here for," Quigley said. "I mean, on such short notice," she said. "Even on short notice," he said. "It's not a trouble for you? Are your children at school?" she said. "I have no children," he said. "And your wife?" she said. "I have no wife. Tell me how I can help" he said. "Now that I'm here I don't know if I can say," she said. "I'm not here to judge you," he said. "I don't know if it's right to," she said. "To confide a sin is not right or wrong," he said. "But what if it's a very bad sin?" she said. "Tell me," he said. "You won't get off on it?" she said. "I don't understand," he said. "I have a thing for men in black," she said. "I understand it's a fashionable color," he said. "And those collars," she said. "My collar?" he said. "I see one on someone like you and it just makes me want to grab it and kiss it and work my mouth down your front to your crotch and take your cock out of your black pants and suck it so hard, that's my sin, Reverend, I confess," she said, and took a couple steps towards him and lifted her skirt. His cell phone buzzed. It was in his pocket not far from the blooming organ to which she made reference. "Sorry," he said, "I'd better take it." He turned a little away and listened. As his features tightened, "Marylou" watched him more intently. He said to the phone that he would be over, that he was a couple towns away but he would be over right away. He had no idea what he would say to her. They looked at each other. "Naked" would be the word for the look between them, if they could even have had a word. "Something's happened," he said.

"Tina, your brother ... he was shot ... I can't say this even ... "

"God! No!" Tina Miles shrieked.

It was a service such as Bealport had seldom seen. There wasn't anyone who wasn't there. Even Billy Hutchins was there, though he wore no tie, because he didn't own one. There were people in the side aisles and in back and out on the sidewalk, with the doors struck open so those on the sidewalk could hear and be a part. The plant closed for an hour. Denise Crosley put the post office flag at half-staff, which may have been against regulations but she did it. Bob Headley received condolences as if almost the loss were his own. No one blamed him. They couldn't see what else he could have done. Nor could he, though the question ate his mind away, not least when the sheriff himself asked it, though there were witnesses, two guys from Ellsworth in a delivery truck, so that was the end of that part of it, the criminal justice part of it. It was lightly raining again, those interminable light rains of a hesitant spring. The rain made everything seem close and one, as if it had happened half a second ago. Tina Miles entered with her parents, whom she held and hugged and helped to find their places. There were those in the church who marked the reconciliation. No one (except the Reverend Quigley) knew her as "Marylou;" many had wondered where she'd disappeared to; there'd been stories; and the one thing people always said was that she should have gone off to New York or one of those, with the talent that girl had. But here she was. So be it.

John Quigley chose the hymns for grandeur and spoke about mystery, both in Christ and in Mikey. He offered the assurances of Heaven, which he felt was only fair, given the circumstances, whether he was personally assured or not. Though at this moment perhaps he was. He was a man who turned this way and that, as though trying to catch up to the world's turnings. Or perhaps better to say the heavens' ins and outs. In the end, at the reception in the light rain, Tina briefly stood beside him. It was enough so that people knew. Burt had a few words with Bob Headley. Burt went up to him. No one knew what was said. Burt and Bev went home alone.

Life would take some getting used to again. You could add "if ever," of course. Bev's prescription so that she could sleep was running low, so Burton went to the Rite Aid for a refill. Everything seemed tentative and futile. Bev closed the door to Mikey's room. Tina would be over later. They would try to be grateful for that much. Bev had in mind to ask her about the Reverend Quigley. Small talk. What other kind was worth having now? When he felt he could leave her for another little while, as she tried busying herself cleaning the kitchen and preparing for Tina, Burton went downstairs to his old Dell. In the chat room of the Winter Soldiers, sympathy for Burton was running high. *Wsstormboy* wanted *wsbealport1* to know that he planned to nominate Mikey as a martyr for the cause. *Wsbigtime88* felt that a strong case could be made for martyrdom, given the nature of the ownership of Norumbega Shoes and the *casus belli* that led Mikey to go over the cliff. *Wsgeorgewashingtonbridge* told *wsbealport1* that if he'd been in Mikey's shoes, and pardon the halfway pun, he damn well might have done the same damn thing, because there's only so much a human being with his dignity can take. *Wsholton* demurred from *wsgeorgewashingtonbridge* on a matter more of procedure than substance, since he felt it was endangering all Winter Soldiers everywhere to say anything online that could be construed by busybodies as some kind of threat, even if in fact it wasn't. *Wsmontauk2* asked about the whole martyr-nominating procedure, as he hadn't heard anything about that before. *Wsstormboy* referred *wsmontauk2* to the pertinent provisions in the Winter Soldier Covenant. *Wslancaster3* told *wsbealport1* flat out that if there were more brave young men like his son in the country, the place would be out of danger by now. Burton read a number more of these, and then, declining to answer any for the moment, he went upstairs to see how Bev was doing in the kitchen.

The Breakfast Hour at the McDonald's

Pete Hammond heard that Roger Keysinger himself had sent Burton and Bev a personal letter. Con Bowden thought it might have been an email, but Pete insisted it was a real letter, on fancy, thick stationery. Always the skeptic, Peg Eaton wanted to know whether Pete had actually seen the stationery, and whether Burton had showed it to him, or otherwise how did he know what it looked like. With some annoyance, Pete told her that Burton had *told* him what it looked like, and it was FedExed up overnight morning delivery, so was she going to go question Burt as well?

It was that kind of morning. People had nothing really to say, so they were irritable. Dawn Smith thought it was a beautiful service and was surprised the Reverend Quigley had it in him. They'd obviously been underestimating the Reverend Quigley in a number of ways, Fox Herman suggested slyly. But most were not in the mood for little jokes about their pastor and Tina Miles. Where *was* that girl living, Marge Deschamps wanted to know. Cathy Maitlin heard it was somewhere near Belfast. But what was she doing over there? Nobody had an answer for that one. Charlie Russell thought she might be working checkout at the Belfast Co-op, which was just a guess but it was as good a one as any, as she'd always been one of those organic people, which engendered the predictable clucking about a talented girl like that.

Thoughts about Mikey were in short supply. Or expressions of thoughts, anyway. Though apropos of what seemed like nothing at all, as if his mind had been wandering all over the sky and just landed, Timmy Thomson smiled and remembered something he'd seen recently on the public station, where one of those pledge week fellas with beards was saying from his research that when something really good happens to somebody, the person thinks it's going to make him happy for a real long time whereas actually it doesn't, the happiness wears off much sooner than he thinks, he overestimates, and by the same token, if something very terrible happens, he's going to think his life's over, whereas that's not true either, people adapt to the new situation even when they never thought they would. That sounded like a man's way of thinking, Cathy Maitland said. She imagined Burt might one day get over it, but Bev never would. Fox Herman stuck up for Timmy: he didn't say people *got over* things, he just said they *adapted*. It was a question of comparative happiness, Timmy said. Those were the words. Comparative happiness. And that's about where things were left.

Shoes

The marketing guys will tell you that they have to have some-thing they can sell. The Norumbega cordovan monk strap, made in America at one of the country's oldest continuously operating shoe factories according to traditional methods and using the finest American shell cordovan, was one such something. Its two-hundred-eighty-two-dollar wholesale cost allowed a retail price point of three hundred ninety-five dollars. Norumbega's Balmoral wingtips, at two hundred fifty-seven dollars wholesale, indicated three hundred sixty dollars in the stores. The line's summer specialty, white bucks brought back for a fashion encore, were the bargain of the lot, at one hundred sixty wholesale, for a store price of two twenty-five, which was a lot for white bucks, according to the marketing folks, but not for a Norumbega shoe, which by June you would be finding in spe-cialty shops from Nantucket to New York to Santa Barbara. And the most upscale of the department stores were sniffing around as well. These were shoes for the rich guy, whether at the yacht club or on Wall Street. The loafers came along for the ride.

How do you sell shoes? You need a story to tell. This was how Roger Keysinger explained the pleasant surprise of orders rolling in to his Madrigal partners in Greenwich. He barged into their offices one by one to gloat. It was still a hobby business, it wasn't big busi-ness, but it was a business. Keysinger would then elaborate. It wasn't only having a story to tell, it was having a product to back the story up. The shoes coming out of Bealport weren't perfect, but they were damn good. And they were comfortable! You didn't have to buy an ugly Nike to give your feet a break. When he was done annoying Kyzlowski and the others, still with his order report in hand, he went to call Bealport. Protocol dictated that he call Vallone first, and then an attaboy for marketing director Hirshhorn, but his real enthusiasm he held in reserve for the call to Billy Hutchins.

KEYSINGER: "Hey, Billy."

BILLY: "Mr. Keysinger?"

KEYSINGER: "You see the order report?"

BILLY: "I did. Yes, sir."

KEYSINGER: "Well kiss our collective asses, am I right?"

BILLY: "Be one way to put it."

KEYSINGER: "You deserve a lot of the credit, Billy. Most of it, really."

BILLY: "Thank you, Mr. Keysinger. Don't know about that, but anyway."

KEYSINGER: "It was your idea. Climb the ladder. Go for the guys with the money."

BILLY: "Long as you've got the product. Long as we could produce."

KEYSINGER: "Well that's where I'm counting on you, to keep delivering."

BILLY: "I'll try, Mr. Keysinger. I'll see what we can do."

KEYSINGER: "And Billy? I'd say, we're officially on first names now. What do *you* say?"

BILLY: "Rog? Sounds a little funny saying it."

KEYSINGER: "Get used to it."

BILLY: "Hey Rog. How's it goin', Rog? Fuck all, Rog."

KEYSINGER: "Fuck yourself, Billy."

BILLY: "Thank you, Rog."

KEYSINGER: "I'm up in a couple weeks. You come over for lunch."

BILLY: "Be my pleasure."

KEYSINGER: "See ya, then."

BILLY: "You too."

KEYSINGER: "Oh and Billy, what do you just think about this? Let me run something by you. Think we could go up another thirty–forty dollars in the pricing?"

BILLY: "Don't see why not. Seems there's some things, the more you charge, the more they can't get enough of."

KEYSINGER: "Of course we don't want to be greedy. We don't want to overplay our hand."

BILLY: "Of course not. Definitely not."

KEYSINGER: "Value for money."

BILLY: "Definitely value for money."

KEYSINGER: "I'll run it by Hirshhorn."

For both men, this conversation was the highlight of their day. Billy Hutchins took it as confirmation that he might after all be a man of affairs. He began thinking of trading up his Beemer, or driving down to Portland and spending a little money on a girl. Rog Keysinger took it as confirmation that he might after all be a man of the people. There was a rollercoaster not far from where he worked, over at Rye Playland. It was an old wooden thing, a national treasure or national landmark or whatever the designation when it's not a building but still worth preserving. He went over that afternoon and rode it a couple times.

Billy didn't make it all the way to Portland, as it began to seem like a long drive, and while he was passing Augusta he saw a place called the Shady Lady. He stopped in for a beer and a dance or two. The girl he chose for the dances looked somewhat familiar but, with all the makeup and eyelashes, he couldn't place the face. In the dark, and with the after-work crowd, she didn't place his either.

The Reward

In the words of Farley Robinson, it was time for some chickens to come home. In the words of Peter Fuller, it was time to get some mileage out of those shoes. In the words of Jim Kyzlowski, it was time to load up. The paltry metaphors of finance, or footwear, or whatever. Only Dick Webber kept quiet, but Dick always did. He was like that Supreme Court justice, Thomas, who never asked a question in twenty years. But when it came for a show of hands, like the others Dick voted for the loan. Keysinger, too, voted for it. He could hardly not. He had promised the others at the beginning that there would be times when they could get their money out. And if not now, when? The quarter had been decent. Orders were coming in. On account of the company's new viability, the interest on the loan would be lower than it would otherwise have been. And debt financing, as always, was tax deductible. On the nineteenth of May, 2006, Madrigal Partners voted unanimously to have their wholly owned subsidiary Norumbega Footwear borrow thirty-one million dollars from State Street Bank, sufficient to pay off the partners' entire original investment and then some.

It was small change, really. It wasn't enough to buy anybody a new plane. But it was enough that the others stopped cursing – which was of course really mock-cursing – Rog Keysinger on account of his damned loafers. All for one and one for all. You couldn't say it often enough.

Keysinger left Greenwich by eleven for the Westchester airport and by noon was on the company jet en route to Santa Fe, where his partners understood there was something new he was looking into. Keysinger was a boy again when he flew. He never got over looking at the tops of clouds. He had a drink and closed his laptop. Even at altitude, when his feet swelled up, his Norumbegas were comfortable. They knew how to breathe. With Madrigal now out from under, he felt once again the leisure of a winner.

Every Seduction Is One Part Premeditation
and One Part Come What May

She said she had some ideas about the shoes and she didn't mean to interfere but would he possibly come down to the Island for an hour and tell her why they were all wrong. It was a request received with a sigh. When you were the Head of Product Development, you didn't say no to the owner's wife. Not anyway the first time she ever called. If it got to be a habit, he'd have to see about it. Besides, going to the Island for an hour gave the possibility that he would see Eliza. He knew her name now. He'd seldom seen her, only three times or four, but he hadn't forgotten her. The deferred dream, the omen of his luck.

There were none of the kids around when Billy drove up the drive. No extra cars, no bikes, no girls with little to do playing croquet or badminton. But if there were no girls there was at least no jerkoff brother either, and for Billy that was close to compensating. Billy had come to the point of view where the thing with the boy had almost never happened. That's why he thought of it as "the thing with the boy." He no longer named it in his mind.

It was the third week in June. It was not a calendar that Billy would have had in mind, but the kids were either still in school or off in distant parts of the globe digging ditches or building yurts to pad their college applications. Courtney had come up to put her garden in. There was no one else around.

Billy was not used to knocking on the front door. Even over the winter, when he was painting alone and there wasn't a soul in five miles to know the difference, he'd still used the side. Courtney was in a white dress a bit too summery for the brisk weather. She looked like she was about to go somewhere. She probably was, Billy thought, off to lunch with her girlfriends at the ramshackle Island Club or to a shopping expedition, though where a woman like Courtney Keysinger would shop in these parts was unclear to him. It was by the way a mystery of the rich to Billy that the Islanders could certainly afford to fix up their shabby-looking clubhouse, but didn't bother. It was almost as if they liked it that way.

Courtney greeted him with a fifties housewife smile, opening the door wide. It was the kind of scene where if Billy'd had a hat on, he would have thought to take it off. But he wasn't wearing a hat. He walked in as if he'd never been in the place before, as if he hadn't had it to himself for most of a month. "You did a nice job upstairs, by the way," she said to break the ice. "Did I ever tell you that?"

"Yes, ma'am, you did, thank you," Billy said.

"I guess that's water under the bridge. A *long* time ago."

Billy recognized that she was referencing his elevation in the world, but he was slow to acknowledge it, sensing the wiser course was to stay humble, which would be best accomplished not with a suspect "Aw shucks" but with pretending not even to have understood.

"Come in my office, would you?" Courtney said, leading him to a room at the end of the house where he'd never been. It was a small room with abundant light from many small-paned windows, book-shelved floor-to-ceiling wherever possible and fitted out with typical home office paraphernalia and decor, to suggest airiness and efficiency, not to say the aspirations of the affluent underemployed. A second director's chair had been pulled up to the long blond-wood desktop on which Courtney had laid out some designs. "Have a seat. Please. I just want you to have a look at these. I want your opinion."

Billy took the seat indicated for him. In front of him, rendered so professionally that he could have been looking at an ad in a magazine, were riffs on the old white buck, namely, yellow bucks, green bucks, rosy bucks, powder blue bucks, navy blue bucks, looking as scrumptious as an array of brightly frosted cupcakes. "Of course I didn't do these myself. I could never have done these myself. I had them done in the city."

"That'd be New York City?" Billy asked, because he didn't know what else to say.

"They're my designs. I did the designs, then took them to New York to have them drawn. Do you want to hear my idea?"

"Sure. Shoot," Billy said, keeping his eyes on the drawings, concentrating, or trying to, however being more or less constantly distracted by the effort to show that he was concentrating.

"My idea is … " Courtney said and hesitated. "Well, you get the idea. It's pretty obvious, isn't it? White bucks are a little dull, a little over, you know what I mean? But people like bucks. So what about bucks in colors? We could do bucks in all these different colors. I mean, *you* could, I didn't mean *I* could. But what do you think?"

"Well, you know, we got those dirty bucks, those brown bucks," Billy said, in a tone that was maybe a shade too diplomatic.

"But they're dull, too!" Courtney said.

"Your typical man tends to like dull, I'd estimate," Billy said.

"Not the men I know," Courtney said, then exclaimed, as though it were an epiphany, "You think they're too gay? I mean the shoes, the shoes are too gay?"

Those wouldn't have been Billy's exact words, but the thought was close enough. It was an area he felt uncomfortable getting into, at least with her. And mostly he didn't want an argument to result.

"Anyway, these are summer shoes. We're already into summer," he said. "I guess that's a problem."

"But what about next summer?" Courtney said.

"We're not up to thinking about next summer yet," Billy said. "Course when the time comes … "

"You'll think about it? You'll consider?"

"Of course. Of course."

"Well that's all I can ask," Courtney said, and she regarded Billy sincerely.

Billy felt he had bought himself some time. They sat there, then

Courtney gathered her drawings from the desk and placed them in a portfolio. She did so silently and with what looked to be hurt feelings.

"It was a terrible idea. I know that," she said. "You don't have to humor me. I told you that when I called you."

"It's not a terrible idea," Billy said, feeling beaten for having to say it.

"It's terrible. It's typical of me," she repeated.

"In a few months. I swear. We'll take a look. We'll pass 'em around. Have you showed your husband?"

"Showed my husband? *Rog*?" It could have been an ice pick she'd put through his name.

"Hey, he's the boss. You get him on your side, you don't need a little guy like me," Billy said.

"You're not a little guy," she said.

"By comparison. You bet I am," he said.

"I don't think so," she said.

She caught his glance and a second or two passed when she didn't let go. It was then Billy realized they were getting into an area he knew a little more about.

Or was he mistaken? Courtney recovered herself. "Would you like a cup of tea? Or I bet you haven't had lunch," she said.

"No lunch, thanks," Billy said.

"I'm sure I could find something."

"Really, no."

"A glass of wine? Oh, that sounds so stupid. A beer?"

"I really ought to be getting back."

"You're afraid of me!"

"No, ma'am. I don't think I am," Billy said.

"The boss's wife, hauls you down here."

"Happy to oblige, ma'am."

"I'll tell you something, Billy. I hired you *first*! I was the one who *found* you!"

"I remember that, Mrs. Keysinger."

"Oh stop that, 'Mrs. Keysinger.' You don't call him *Mis*-ter Keysinger, do you?"

"Only he insisted."

"Well what do you think *I'm* doing?"

"All right, I'll have a beer," Billy said. His hope was for an interval to calm her down. She got up and came back, with a Heineken for him, because foreign beers were all they had, and a glass of Burgundy for herself.

"I take it you don't want a glass."

"Whatever. Fine."

"Why do people like you not want a *glass*?"

"People like me?"

"I mean, like in the movies, or TV. They're always, like, *guzzling*. I don't mean *you*."

It did occur to Billy who did she mean if not him, but what was the point to dispute. She was a goofball. This was his judgment. He just hadn't spent enough time with her to be one hundred percent conclusive before.

Though Courtney saw things rather differently. If she was a goofball, he was her James Dean. She reached out with her wine glass, as if to recover her balance with a toast. Billy flicked the bottom of his bottle towards her glass. Their conversation then settled into a more conventional chat, much as he had hoped for. About this and that, the factory and shoes in general and Bealport and the Island. Courtney found enough things to say. Billy nodded a lot and was careful not to go too far wrong, aware that in his own ways he was as clueless as she was. He was about to opine, for instance, about the crappy state of the Island Club and how they ought to really do something to fix it up and he knew of several fellas who could do the work if price was the issue, but then he wondered if that was really being helpful, to suggest they were too cheap to pay the going rate.

She saved him from his mistake, in order, Billy would later think, to make her own. "The reason I don't show my husband these designs, if you really want to know, is that he wouldn't be interested."

"Now why would that be? He bought the factory," Billy said.

"Oh, he's interested in *shoes*. He's interested in *shoes*, all right. He's just not interested in *me*!"

"Ma'am, you're telling me things, I'm really not sure … "

"Would you fucking stop 'ma'am'ing me! Just stop! Courtney! *Me*! Stop!"

"Sorry."

The two director's chairs were angled more at each other than they had been. Courtney folded up into hers, so crumpled it was as if she no longer needed the whole chair. Billy could hardly remember the woman he'd met in the garden, it was like the butterfly had become a caterpillar again, life grinding its gears into reverse. She said, bitterly, but how else, "You know where he is now? Have you heard from him? I don't even know. He's got a new girlfriend. Not *a* girlfriend. A *new* girlfriend. Believe me, there've been others. At those conferences? You know why he doesn't take me? That's all they are, they're fuck-fests!"

"Is he at a conference?"

"I don't know where the fuck he is!"

"I'm sorry to hear all this … "

"*Ma'am*? Were you going to say '*ma'am*'?"

"Ma'am … "

"*Ma'am? Ma'am?*"

"Ma'am!"

At least they had that little laugh together. Little hiccups, back and forth. Courtney unfolded herself then. "I liked you the first time I saw you," she said.

"Hey, I like you," he said.

"You don't get it, do you?" she said.

"I get you're a little pissed at Rog."

She reached across and put a hand on his. The truth was that Billy had always had a low level of resistance to such things. Tears messed her mascara. She may have been a handsome woman, but with the melting of her eyes and the patches of redness here and there and everywhere and her facial lines that now looked more hardened and fixed to a final unhappiness, Billy became afraid to look. To really look, that is. All he wanted to see was her daughter, Eliza. Was she in there somewhere, anywhere?

They screwed on the Isfahan of newly bright natural-dye colors on the floor, for of course the home office of one of the affluent underemployed would have a newly bright natural-dye Isfahan there. Throughout the act, even when his eyes were open enough, he saw only Eliza in his mind. What a thrill she would be, what a love! Eliza in her black bathing suit, Eliza taking it off, Eliza on the floor with him. Courtney moaned, still in her white dress, and afterwards Billy would feel that he had showed her a very good time.

The Shoot

Hirshhorn had the idea to dip a toe into web advertising. Somebody from an Ann Arbor firm had cold-called him and convinced him it was so cheap they could hardly go wrong. Hirshhorn thought to himself, we could be pioneers, we could be on the cutting edge, leap-frogging ahead, the way, for example, that you heard in some foreign countries people who had never had a telephone at all now had cell phones. So, in order that Norumbega not be left behind in the dustbin of history, a minimal camera crew duly arrived from Portland for a "shoot." The unlikelihood of the whole thing might have been indicated by those quotation marks, which resided in the minds of a majority of the Norumbega workers when they heard about it, but it didn't stop Billy from buying a new sweater and some pants from the L.L. Bean outlet and a couple items for Earl, so that they would look appropriately country but not inappropriately unwashed country for the camera. Earl was to be the focal point. Earl the master shoemaker, passing his skill, his lore, his unerring old-Maine taste, a composite of the woods and the Puritans, on to the younger generation, represented by Billy.

But not Gary. Gary was one too many actors for the plot. He and half the factory floor looked on or at least stole glances while this careful airbrushing of Earl's current capacities and contributions was committed to its thirteen minutes of posterity. What a crock, was what you might have heard Con Bowden appraising under his breath to Timmy Thompson, expressing the general good-natured skepticism. Gary was less amused but didn't say so. His good-natured skepticism was feigned, he was boiling up with resentment and hurt, folding and unfolding his arms as if all this standing around were one long restless night, looking on and turning away and stealing a glance again.

The shoot took through the morning. For the first hour, Earl had the frozen deer look of someone who'd never had his picture taken in his life. Billy loosened him up with a little Jim Beam in the back room. It was possible that Earl had faked his discomfort simply in order to induce this result.

There were both stills and a bit of video. For both of them Billy and Earl sat in ladder back chairs looking straight out to nowhere as if they were auditioning for *American Gothic*. The only real movement was when one or the other of them raised a shoe for the camera.

The dialogue for the video:

EARL *(picking up a worn-looking but serviceable loafer)*: "This here particular shoe we made in 1934 and it's still on its feet."

BILLY: "On somebody's feet."

EARL: "Correct. Somebody's. Who wears it on a daily basis, this individual. Now if you added it up, you'd think he'd be croaked by now, this individual."

BILLY: "But he's not?"

EARL: "It's his son, stupid. Best part of his inheritance."

BILLY *(holding up a burnished cordovan monk strap)*: "And here's a new/old style, made in our factory here in Bealport, Maine by thirty-seven different pairs of hands this very day … "

EARL: "For certain you mean *yesterday* … "

BILLY: "The master shoemaker speaks … "

EARL: "Don't be dissing your old man now. I say that right, 'dissing?'"

BILLY *(turning the shoe so it can be seen)*: " … made right here by thirty-seven different pairs of hands *yesterday* … "

EARL *(interrupting)*: "My point is only, if it was bein' done this very day, how could you be showin' it to 'em?"

BILLY: " … using the most premium cordovan leathers in the world. Norumbega Footwear's been making fine American shoes for more than a hundred years."

EARL: "So buy 'em and put 'em in your will."

BILLY: "You know, Dad, that's kind of a morbid thought."

EARL: "Just suggestin'."

There was never a take when Earl was completely on his lines. It wasn't so much incapacity or the Jim Beam, but that he simply refused. Billy was better, hinting to the crew that he had some experience, unspecified, in that area. By noon the director felt she had something she could put together, and they were due in Portland at three for a used car commercial, so they left. Earl felt that once he'd got going, he'd improved the thing with his "ad libs," and expressed himself that if they didn't want his creative contributions, why'd they ask him in the first place?

When they were done and the last lingering employees had drifted back to work, Billy saw that Courtney Keysinger was sitting on the metal stairs up to the executives, squinched over so that people could get by her but at a high enough elevation to have been observing the shoot. She had her portfolio at her side. It wasn't a sight Billy welcomed. Since their encounter, he'd experienced the predictable amounts of self-incrimination, culminating in thinking he was an idiot. Live dangerously or not at all? Yeah, well, maybe. Or, not this time. What an old bag she was, to Billy's now-wary, even frightened, eye. Oh Eliza! What ever happened to her? Courtney waved. Billy waved back, still hoping he could avoid her by wandering off on the factory floor, making his rounds. But she waved a second time, this time for him to come to her. He took the stairs in a hurry, to suggest this had best be brief. Courtney chose not to take the bait.

COURTNEY: "Hi."

BILLY: "How are you, Mrs. Keysinger?"

COURTNEY: "Very well, thank you, Mr. Hutchins."

BILLY: "Sorry. Runnin' around a little. You see the thing?"

COURTNEY: "The commercial? It was funny."

BILLY: "You thought so?"

COURTNEY: "Absolutely. Good luck with it."

BILLY: "Only for the internet. Four people'll see it."

COURTNEY: "Who knows? Maybe not. I think it's *marvelous*

you're embracing those things. Listen, Mr. Hutchins, could I steal ten minutes of your time?"

BILLY: "You know with that filming and everything, I'm running a little behind … "

COURTNEY: "Just ten minutes."

BILLY *(a grimace, not quite suppressed)*: "Come on. Let's have it. Sure. Of course."

Then they were in Billy's office, enclosed in glass, but with the door shut.

BILLY *(her portfolio in front of him, turning pages of new renderings)*: "What would I be looking at exactly, Mrs. Keysinger?"

COURTNEY: "You're looking at my new ideas, Mr. Hutchins. I thought, why not *saddle shoes*? If we did the offsetting colors, like, look, the red with the blue? They wouldn't have to be for the summer."

BILLY: "They still look pretty summery to me."

COURTNEY: "Even in the darker colors?"

BILLY: "Look, we're going to consider all these. Definitely we are. I promise you."

COURTNEY *(low)*: "He's in Jackson Hole with that whore."

BILLY: "I said we'd consider all these in due time, Mrs. Keysinger. Really, I think that's the right course. They're wonderful. They're fabulous."

COURTNEY *(low)*: "You were pretty wonderful yourself."

BILLY: "Why don't you let me keep these, Mrs. Keysinger, and then when it's time … "

COURTNEY *(low)*: "I know, it's inappropriate for me to say these things, for me to come in here, be a pest, I'm sorry, really, we never have to do this again, you clearly don't want to, I mean it couldn't be more apparent, so if that's how you feel, I'm not forcing you, *Mis-ter Hutchins*."

BILLY: "I really got to get over to the finishing department, Mrs. Keysinger. You know how it goes, when the master's away … "

COURTNEY *(low)*: "When he's away following his dick all over the country … Why do you hate me?"

BILLY: "Thanks for coming in, Mrs. Keysinger. We really appreciate your interest."

COURTNEY *(low)*: "Fuck you."

But at least she left. Nor did she "storm out." She had good sense enough not to, but simply left, with her portfolio still on Billy's old desk, a reminder, a wide stain that would not come out easily. He closed the cover of the portfolio, took a breath, busied himself until she was gone, then descended the metal stairs to make his rounds. It then occurred to him to consider the possibility that there really might be something to Courtney's new designs. Saddle shoes could work most of the year. He'd never seen such colors before. And so what if they were too gay? Those people bought a lot of shoes. You didn't need some market research genius to know that much.

The conversation between Billy and Courtney in Billy's office, the dynamics of it, the body language and expressions that accompanied it, went largely unnoticed as the factory picked up where it left off. Really, only Gary Hutchins noticed. He saw Billy and Mrs. Keysinger climb the stairs together. He followed. He pretended business upstairs, got a drink of water, and looked. He could tell it wasn't a pretty picture, but beyond that, who could know? It was bad enough, in terms of Gary's feelings, that Billy was on speaking terms with the boss's wife.

Clear Sailing

It was something, to be doing well enough, to see the future clearly enough, to buy a big boat. Kristen wanted a sailboat, because after all Sean could sail – he'd had a "scholarship" to the Island Club's sailing program when he was eleven and twelve years old – and because sailing was so aimless and rich, or it seemed that way, anyway, to someone standing on the shore. Sailing made you one of *them.* Whereas Sean had a somewhat different take, in that he didn't want to be one of them, he was a simpler soul than she was, he only wanted to go faster than them. Or as fast as, if he couldn't go faster, if it could cost him his job to go faster. Sean's father once explained the universe to him based on the General Motors hierarchy of cars. Chevrolet, you were just starting out. Pontiac, you were still young but coming up and wanted something a little sportier to show it. The Olds, middle-level management. Buick, upper-level management. Cadillac, the boss. Something like that. Sean, you could say, wanted Pontiac speed and Buick respectability. He wanted a power boat and that's what they got, a 28-foot Grady-White with three Yamaha 225 four-strokes yoked together, which was way more than the Grady-White needed, which was how he wanted it. Kristen was more accustomed to looking up at the world. Sean was more partial to looking down. You could either spot a mismatch here or say that they had the world covered. They bought the boat in May and spent the long days of June, weekend days, spraying great wakes up and down the bay. Everyone in Bealport could see them. It was one thing to wave at people you passed on the water. Everyone did it even if no one knew why. But Sean and Kristen took to waving at people on the dock or on the land. There were people in Bealport who made light of this. Some things you can get away with and some things you can't. Con Bowden was partial to telling people the boat wasn't secondhand, it was thirdhand.

Meanwhile Billy spent his good fortune on a "rice rocket," a totaled '94 Honda Civic which he planned to un-total. The Derby would be coming up again. Billy's theory was that despite a long history of Japanese cars getting hammered in the Derby, a small, agile car if properly handled might still outlast a lumbering giant, might skirt around and evade, might pull off an improbable Ali, floating like a butterfly and stinging like a bee, might beat Gary at his own rope-a-dope game. For it was of course Gary who was Billy's target. Years ago the two had competed, before Billy went west, and Gary always won. At the time, Billy resented it, but not any more. Now, if he thought about it, he began to pity Gary, for those wins being the furthest he would go in life. Though Billy wasn't really mean enough to pity, and moreover if he'd pitied, he would have ceased wanting to win. But Billy wanted to win, wanted to show his brother on his brother's terms. It was a reflex that never went away.

And besides, the Derby was fun. He rented space in the back of Ed Morrison's garage, and paid Ed a bit extra for the use of his tools as might be needed, and went to work a couple nights a week with a couple of beers for company. He knew cars because every kid who grew up in Bealport knew cars. He added to it and subtracted from it and snuck in secret steel so that soon you would hardly guess he had started with a '94 Civic. It looked more like a shrunk Hummer.

Gary didn't care that Billy was entering the Derby, but about everything else he did care. The strutting around the plant that didn't look like strutting around, that looked more like a guy just walking around, but a little too fast, so that if you looked close you could tell how much he thought of himself, as if the whole world would likely go to hell if it didn't get his immediate attention. Then that ad, that waste-of-time stupid ad, that could have been making fun of all of them, Gary wasn't sure of it, but it could have been. Gary told himself even if Billy had put him in it, if it had been all three of them up there, the shoemaking Hutchinses of Bealport, it wouldn't have made a difference to his feelings. And then there was the parade of Beemers, the older one, the newer one. And how could it have happened that now Billy talked to the boss's wife as if they were on an equal situation in life?

Other things, more things: just the sight of Billy, or people talking about him, acting as if whatever he said was some kind of authority, hearing about Billy's antics, hearing about something he'd bought or some new idea he had as if it was going to be the next Noah's Ark. It kept Gary up nights. It disrupted his sleep and churned his digestion and made him not want to go to work for having to hear or see more of it. It made him sad and irritable. Even Jerome began to notice, how little his dad had to say at dinner, how he seemed to be distracted by something, so that you could say things to him and most of the time he heard as usual but sometimes he didn't. Martha had some inklings, but because Gary was embarrassed by his jealousy and kept all but a percent or two of the iceberg of it out of sight, she wasn't sure, and she dared not ask, for fear of humiliating him further.

Gary wasn't much for stationery, but he did have a pad from the NAPA store, and it was on this one night that he wrote the following:

Dear Mr. Keysinger,

This would be something to go in the suggestion box but I dont believe we have such a one operating at the present time. Your employee William Hutchins worked previusly at Norumbega but was fired by his employer Mr and Mrs Berman at that time for selling drugs i.e. cocaine on the premisses. If you check with them, you'll know. They are I believe in Naples, Florida.

A Concerned employee

When he was done writing, Gary felt he'd taken action to address his fate. Which was a Cadillac way to say it, possibly, but he could begin to breathe again, and walk around, and not be afraid, of himself or anything else, but mostly of himself. You can only take so much, Gary thought. But then he thought, NAPA stationery with the NAPA car parts logo on it was not the right way to send a letter to the president of the company. So the next evening he borrowed Jerome's computer and got Jerome to set up the correct programs for him and Gary pecked out what he wanted to say. Gary was au courant with the computer as far as investigating a bit of web, but less familiar with it as a tool of composition. He understood what certain icons indicated, for example, yet was pleasantly surprised by whatever it was that corrected the words he spelled wrong. Jerome then printed the thing out for him on a clean white sheet of paper. Gary stood by the printer in such a way that Jerome wouldn't see what was on the sheet of paper. He put the letter in one of Martha's envelopes for paying bills and addressed it to Mr. Roger Keysinger in Connecticut and stamped the envelope, all of it as though he were getting a child ready to send out into the world.

But at the post office, in front of the slot, from which it was well known that nothing could ever be retrieved, it being the iron law of the United States Postal Service that once it was in there it wasn't yours anymore but theirs to faithfully deliver, Gary abruptly tore up what he had written. He tore it up into so many pieces that even if Denise went rummaging around in the blue post office trash bin to see what was what among her customers, she couldn't have easily put back together what Gary wrote. Gary even tore up the stamp.

The TV Scene

It's often in a bathroom, the person curled up or stretched out, paraphernalia scattered around, tourniquet on the arm, something gone wrong. The man or the woman perhaps not quite unconscious, perhaps mumbling or muttering something, signage to all those watching at a distance: don't go here. We've all seen it on TV, a few times or a dozen or a hundred, depending on the frequency and taste of our television consumption. Why even bother describing it again? There's something even a little obscene about describing it again, the mechanicalness of it, the obligatoriness of it, the piety. God save George Keysinger, a sweet kid, with his red hair, from our piety. He was only trying to do what his brother did, after all. Only trying to keep up. George Keysinger, age sixteen, of Greenwich, CT, was discovered early this morning overdosed of heroin and taken to Eastern Maine Medical Center. It's not exactly how the story might have run in the paper, but close enough. But nothing appeared in the paper.

It was Eliza who found him. The girls shared one bathroom and the boys another, but Mary as usual was hogging up the girls', so Eliza went down the hall, knocked, entered, and found him. She thought he was dead at first. She was inconsolable. The Downeast Ambulance came. The paramedics were not unfamiliar with the drug-sick. They administered the Narcan on the ride to Bangor.

Hamilton Keysinger felt appropriately remorseful. Courtney Keysinger sat appropriately by George's bedside at the hospital. Rog Keysinger appropriately flew back from wherever he was.

The Spark of Life

Pledge week, in Martha Hutchins' ratings of the sad inevitabilities of life, ranked somewhere between an early frost before the last of her tomatoes had ripened and going to the dentist for a scaling. There was no escaping it. Or of course there was. She could sit there and rank the sad inevitabilities of life. She could click-click-click the remote in search of something not altogether cruel or gross on the commercial channels. She could go downstairs and bake a pie. Or she could shelter in place and be pleaded with, even after she'd sent in her twenty-five dollars, by actors who'd had too many facelifts or singers who had no voice left. Martha did send in her twenty-five dollars, because she felt it was only right. If you watched, why shouldn't you pay? They had a point with that one. But it didn't mean she was satisfied with the pledge week programming. Too much for the old folks. All those show tunes, all that black-and-white film. Not that Martha wasn't partial to some of the old show tunes, that sang themselves in her head at the oddest times, the way volunteers showed up in her garden. But they played the same ones year after year. It was worse than re-runs. Re-runs, at least in general, you'd only seen once or maybe twice before. And then there was that whole issue of feeling like old folks. Without a doubt there was a significant portion of the population who would consider Martha "old folks," but she wasn't a part of them. They didn't know what she felt like inside, she would say, the way others would say. Martha herself didn't know what she felt like inside most of the time, but if there was one thing that she and whatever was down there could agree on, it was that she was not too damn old. Not for a lot of things. Though naming what those things were exactly was another matter. Being a mother, that was one. She was far from being a grandmother, which was when you were really old. And the spark of life?

"The Spark of Life" was the name of the program that was on the public station the night that young George Keysinger was found passed out on the Island. Self-help shows were another staple of pledge week that Martha could have done with a lot less of, especially the ones which were about getting rich, where you could see the people in the audience almost salivating. Martha didn't believe those salivating people would be getting too rich anytime soon, and likewise the audiences on the shows where the guy had you thinking that if you kept your mind active you wouldn't get dementia, or if you ran a mile a day you wouldn't get a heart attack, or if you cut out the bacon you wouldn't get cancer, all those audiences looked to her to be one hundred percent too gullible and eager. It seemed like whenever the camera looked their way, every third or fourth person was nodding "yes" as if what they were really thinking was "amen." Were all these people hearing things the man hadn't exactly said, or was he really saying them but in a sort of haze, and they were hearing through the haze? Raising false hopes. Martha was way against raising false hopes.

Which happened to be exactly what the host of "The Spark of Life," an Indian named Ravi Banerjee, was warning against, the tendency of a person in his position to raise false hopes and the need for people in the position of the audience not to let people in his position get away with it. Ravi Banerjee could have been reading her mind. He was a slender young man with dark hair combed back and an expressive nose. He sat on a stool with a microphone and didn't move around like the preachers and hucksters did, nor did he wave at his listeners or exhort them. His voice was so mellow that you could wonder, if it wasn't for the microphone, if anybody would hear him. Martha even turned the sound up on the remote, as he began listing all the false hopes that people had: that they would live forever, that they would become rich, that they would be on the cover of a magazine, that they would find the perfect mate and never have a quarrel or a doubt, that their children would love them unconditionally. Martha had to admit that she had had all of these hopes. She tried to make them into a list in her brain, so that she wouldn't forget. Because they *were* false, weren't they? Maybe not always, but most of the time. Banerjee admitted that some people got lucky. But luck was not the same as fate.

What did *that* mean, luck was not the same as fate? Martha's eyes narrowed. She felt she ought to be able to understand the things that people said on the television, and that when she didn't it was either the-person-who-said-it's fault or her own. The television wasn't like books, after all. If it was a book she was reading, Martha would expect not to understand. But then Banerjee explained, as if he could almost read her mind: luck was short-term, fate was forever.

Once you saw it like that, you could see that even if people were lucky, they could still have false hopes. Luck didn't change the larger picture. Martha opened the bag of cheesy popcorn that accompanied her pledge week watching and wondered if she had been lucky in life or not. It was hard to know, there being so many things she could count on each side of the ledger, and enough additional ones where she had no idea which side of the ledger they belonged on. It was about half past eight in the evening when Martha opened her bag of popcorn. It was ten-fifteen when Gary walked in from the garage. Pledge Week was on to Roy Orbison now.

Martha had difficulty ever keeping a secret, so the first thing she said to him, after muting the Roy Orbison, was, "I'm going away for a weekend. You'll have to take care of Jerome." Gary assumed she meant going to see her sick aunt up in Millinocket. There weren't too many left on the Pierce side and Aunt Delle was a favorite of Martha's. "Delle hit a bad patch?" he replied.

But it wasn't Aunt Delle she was going to see, nor was it an emergency situation for the coming weekend or the next. Martha almost felt giddy to tell him. It was so unlike her. It was totally unlike her. "I'm going for a retreat. In September. In Peterborough, New Hampshire."

Gary was unsure, to begin with, exactly what a "retreat" was. It sounded like camping. You heard about business retreats, which weren't exactly camping, but Martha wouldn't be going to a business retreat. Martha observed him hesitating. But she told herself that at least he didn't faint.

"You ever been to New Hampshire before?" he asked tentatively. "I guess you take 95 down there."

"It's not about the route, Gary, it's about the retreat! Don't you want to hear about it?"

"Sure. Go ahead. Tell me," he said, showing not exactly the pinnacle of enthusiasm but within the range up or down of what she might have been expecting.

So she turned off the television altogether and, feeling liberated from the mute grainy images of concerts long ago, proceeded to tell him her understanding of false hopes, Ravi Banerjee, and the spark of life. Like the TV program, it's what the weekend retreats were called, Sparks of Life, and they were having one in New Hampshire but they were all around the country. The idea was for people to examine all their false hopes, and once they'd examined them, they could begin to be free of them, and once they were free of them, that's when they could see the spark of life in themselves, which was so little and quiet that the false hopes got in the way of even knowing it was there. But your spark of life was your real hope. And Mr. Banerjee was saying don't place any false hopes in him, either, not any more than in anyone or anything else, it was something you had to find out for yourself. She liked that part in particular.

Martha was aware that this could sound like malarkey, and she could see it on Gary's face, but instead of retreating or getting all defensive, which is what she usually did when Gary gave her that look about one thing or another to say what a load of crap, she felt a weird spirit to go for it. "Ravi Banerjee's going to be there himself," she added.

"Oh is he now?" Gary said, though he cut his sarcasm with a sweet enough smile.

"He is," Martha said.

"So how much this thing cost, this retreat?" Gary said.

"This is something I want to do," Martha said.

"I hear that," Gary said. "But just give us a ballpark here, would you be so kind, Missus Hutchins?"

"I put a two hundred dollar deposit down," Martha said.

"You already gave 'em money?" Gary said.

"I had to. Otherwise there might not have been a place," Martha said.

Now, two hundred dollars was not small change in the Hutchins household. They had in the bank only nineteen hundred dollars, and this was before certain taxes were due and there was of course money owed on the card. Martha knew this as well as Gary.

All Gary could think was that she'd never done such a thing before, she'd always been more or less the sweet soul of reason, so how could he deny her going batshit this first and only time? Not that she was about to be denied. It didn't look like she could be. But what was going on?

Gary was so perplexed that he didn't even ask how much more was due. A two hundred dollar deposit, right on the card, just like that. But then he remembered the times he'd come home with the hulk of a '76 Caprice or a worn-out trooper car, and they were in the same price range really. He began to feel grateful that Martha hadn't brought those into the discussion. But of course she could, she might still. She looked so unexpectedly happy, like the time she won in the lottery. This too was perplexing to him. You could normally figure when Martha would be happy. In the lottery she'd won nine hundred.

The Protégé

It didn't take long for it all to come out. A few days of rehab, a couple hours of family therapy. The prescribed, maybe obligatory, rite of passage. Tell all, start over, maybe tell all again, maybe start over again. But the Keysingers weren't at the maybes yet. Everything was going to turn out all right. Courtney had done her shopping thing and they had the "best" rehab money could buy. Rog stuck around Connecticut so as to be at every session. George had stuck a needle in his arm only once and never would again. Ham confessed all, but none of it would get back to Choate or onto his Dartmouth application. Recovery was the name of the game, even if it really was a game.

Billy felt the chances were decent that his name would never come into it. After all, "the thing with the boy" was a year ago and it happened only one time. Weighing the situation, you could imagine that this kid George getting sick might have had nothing to do with his brother at all, that the older kid would even be extra careful now not to let a thing about himself get out. Or even if it got out, who knew what kind of a drug fiend this Hamilton Keysinger was? Billy's name could be one of a hundred, in terms of all his suppliers. He wasn't going to go naming a hundred names. It could be like on the interstate, where everybody's speeding but the cop only gets one or two. Or zebras. Billy was aware that lions ate zebras but most zebras got out alive. So when Tim Vallone called him to his office, Billy was fully prepared to talk about what had been recently on his mind, namely, that he'd been thinking over Courtney's idea for saddle shoes, or two-color bucks, or whatever you felt to call them, bucks in bright colors, and the conclusion Billy had come to was that the boss's wife was onto something.

Vallone was in a businesslike mood, but that was not exceptional for Vallone. In Billy's opinion, Vallone did businesslike in order to avoid having to have a personality. The brief dialogue between them:

VALLONE *(gesturing predictably)*: "Have a seat."

BILLY: "Sure. What's going on? You hear anything about Rog's kid?"

VALLONE: "He's doing all right. He's doing fine. Funny you should ask, though."

BILLY: "How's that?"

VALLONE: "Billy, you're terminated. As of immediately. As of right now. Orders of Mr. Keysinger."

BILLY: "I want to speak to the man. That's crazy. That's nuts. Why?"

VALLONE: "Do you really want me to go into it?"

BILLY: "I just don't have a clue what you're saying here."

VALLONE: "You introduced heroin into the boss's family. How's that? You could have killed his kid."

BILLY: "Who said that? Just tell me who said it. That's not a hundred percent lie, it's a thousand percent."

VALLONE: "You've got an hour to be off the premises."

BILLY: "I'm not gonna get fired for something I didn't do. Who said it? I've gotta talk to Rog."

VALLONE: "Mr. Keysinger particularly stated that he doesn't want to talk to you."

BILLY: "He's hiding behind you then? You're his mouthpiece?"

VALLONE *(to intercom)*: "Cherie, could you have Bob Headley come up here? On the double, please."

BILLY *(re the call to security)*: "Oh, now that's low. That's really low. Hey, don't get your period, Timmy, I'm on my way. I don't stay where I'm inconveniencing folks. Just have Rog give me a call."

VALLONE: "You call him if you think he's your big pal."

BILLY *(standing, at the door)*: "Funny thing is, I was coming in here with the best idea we had yet. Tell that to Rog, would you?"

Billy departed Vallone's office in ample time before Bob Headley arrived. He had nothing in his desk to clean out, nor goodbyes to say, and was gone from the whole place in fifteen minutes. He did try Rog Keysinger, several times, on every number Rog had provided him, but Keysinger neither picked up the phone nor replied to Billy's messages. Soon enough, because it was his disposition, Billy was mordantly looking for the consolation prize in his new situation. This was in his Beemer as he drove seventy out onto the county road. He found it in the confidence that Keysinger would never call the sheriff, as that would drag his boys in.

If he had known, Billy might have found further solace in Keysinger's reaction to his protégé's betrayal. Just to say that phrase, "protégé's betrayal," fairly much says it all. Keysinger wasn't just enraged at Billy. His feelings were hurt. His self-love was at risk. He called into question his own judgment. His mouth felt dry, with a metallic aftertaste, as if his whole body was out of whack. Part of this of course had to do with his younger son's narrow escape from death, which in rehab they made a point to say it was. But on his feet, Rog Keysinger's Norumbega loafers were not as comfortable as they'd been. He was damned if he was going to miss Billy.

The Sleepless Night

Gary's mind felt like it was coming at him from all directions. He tried to think of one thing but thought another. He considered that he was a coward, for not sending the letter, but at the same time being glad he hadn't sent it, but at the same time as well being glad that Billy was fired. He was fairly sure he was more glad for Billy being fired than he would have been glad for himself if he'd been promoted or gotten a big raise. What kind of man thinks such thoughts?

But the gladness didn't go away. It was a gladness that nipped at his heels, that chased him now in circles and now in a long straight flight, as if it were the gladness of a hellhound.

Martha slept beside him, snoring away, secure in her spark of life. There were moments that night when Gary resented her as well.

An Announcement

Already in Connecticut for George's therapy, Keysinger met with his partners at Madrigal. He called the meeting himself. Kyzlowski was on vacation but they set up a video conference link from the Grande Bretagne in Athens. Keysinger thanked everybody for their kind thoughts and wishes about his son, who he said was about ninety-nine percent recovered and only had a week to go before he'd graduate with stars on his forehead. But as for the business at hand. His partners noticed that Rog was agreeably cheerful. Was it another case of the old saw so often quoted by B-school guys, whatever knocks me makes me stronger? Rog looked like he'd shed a care. And what was that care? The tall man from Missouri leaned back with his head cradled in his hands as if he was about to tell a pretty good joke. He said he hadn't lost sleep over it, it was simply a fact, he no longer wanted to be in the shoe business. Perhaps no one else noticed, but the camera feeding Jim Kyzlowski's link in Athens had either slipped or was aimed poorly, so that Kyzlowski could observe Rog Keysinger wearing big white Nikes on his size twelve and a half feet.

The announcement came, more or less simultaneously, in the form of a notice to each worker and a press release. Tim Vallone got a heads-up phone call, fifteen minutes before the news went out. The press release stated that on the fifth of August, 2006, Madrigal Partners announced that as of the first of September, 2006, it would be closing the operations of Norumbega Footwear, the one-hundred-and-three-year-old manufacturer of fine men's footwear in Bealport, Maine. The press release cited, as reasons for the closure, the intensity of foreign competition in the footwear industry, the difficult cost structure for producing shoes in America, and consumers' changing tastes. Madrigal, the release said, had made a valiant and persistent effort to overcome these difficulties since acquiring Norumbega, and was proud of its all-American workforce which produced a product second to none. The U.S. Department of Labor would be sending its Rapid Response Team to help Norumbega's employees with job retraining.

The notice each worker received was signed personally by Rog Keysinger, was addressed personally to the worker, contained a statement of heartfelt thanks and regrets in addition to the facts stated in the press release, and specified the number of weeks, based on length of service, that each worker's severance package would consist of. That number of weeks could be as many as sixteen and as few as two.

The Breakfast Hour at the McDonald's

The first disagreement to break out was between Fox Herman and Timmy Thomson over who was to blame. Timmy said not that it mattered but they never should have let Billy in there in the first place, with all his big ideas, running around like he was, and with his dealing out drugs, he should have been in the state penitentiary some time ago and not the executive suite. "You call that the executive suite?" Marge Deschamps hooted, but it was Fox who made the argument back at Timmy: not that it mattered – he agreed with that much – but it was Roger Keysinger who had the piss poor judgment to hire Billy in the first place. Keysinger was a phony and Billy was a phony, so what did you expect, observed Carl Esposito, who was one of those who lost his job in the first round of layoffs and so could be thought to have a more objective view of things, a certain amount of perspective due to the elapse of time.

Martha, who for whatever reasons spoke less in the mornings than some of the others, mentioned the possible fact she heard that it wasn't Billy who was dealing the drugs but Matt Farnsworth and Billy was just like the mule or whatever they call that person in the middle.

Charlie Russell felt that was interesting information but irrelevant.

Dawn Smith put in that this boy, the Keysinger boy, could have died. Oh now wasn't that just too bad, an angry Pete Hammond said, but Dawn, for a change, held her ground. Whatever he deserved for the way he was behaving, he was only a boy, she said. It could have been that Pete then felt ashamed of himself. Dawn said she certainly hoped so.

An uncomfortable silence followed this divergence from the day's central concern. Peggy Eaton and Con Bowden obligingly filled it by disagreeing as to what the chances were that still another buyer could be found for the business. Con's point was that the current owners Madrigal hadn't even put the place up for sale, for whatever reasons, and his understanding was that you couldn't have a buyer if you didn't have a seller. Peggy's point was that Con's point was incredibly stupid even if he was being sarcastic, and that of course if a buyer came forward, why wouldn't Madrigal want to sell, and moreover they should all of them sitting there never forget that Norumbega had been going through thick and thin for longer than their own lives, a lot of their parents had worked there as well as themselves, so they shouldn't be giving up hope yet. Peg was thus fulfilling her role as Bealport historian. Doing her patriotic duty, so to speak. But the others didn't seem convinced.

They settled into another difficult silence. It was a morning when people simply had less to say. Instead of the usual morning chatter, there were these occasional eruptions, spurts of lava that would go on for seconds or minutes and then abruptly the flow would stop. A sullen mood had taken hold, composed of that old troika that was like a Christmas card in reverse, hurt, anger, and fear. You could almost hear people eating their breakfasts, those who were even eating breakfast. The words "unemployment" and "layoffs" were scarcely spoken, though Cathy Maitland did allow that she would be welcoming those people from the Rapid Response Team, a remark which earned a repressed grumble of laughter from Pete Hammond.

Nothing was going to change, Burton Miles said, apropos of what exactly no one could say. Nor did anyone challenge Burt these days, as if, no matter their own griefs and crises, his, not a year gone by, was still paramount. Burton of course felt the same – what was losing a job once you'd lost a son? But for all these other people, his friends, the people he'd known in life, though he wished to, he couldn't find the words. None of them could, really. The workers of Norumbega footwear swung between uncertainty and fatality, then went off to work, still swinging.

A Dialogue in Gary's Garage

It was a distraction surely to have the Derby two weeks away, to be out in the garage till all hours, to be fixing up the Lincoln once again. New old tires, new old scrapyard parts, the secret steel snuck here and there, which of course wasn't exactly to the rules but everybody did it, and it could be argued that once or twice the secret steel had saved a life. Two hundred fifty invested, maybe a little more. Norumbega was closing, but Gary willed himself not to think about the money. If he thought about the money, there'd be nothing left at all.

On the Thursday evening following the announcement, Earl showed up on his Harley. Gary figured it was to use his tools. Gary had tools, Earl had none. But it wasn't that at all.

EARL *(his lament)*: "Damned if that wasn't the unfairest thing. The boy didn't know what he was doing. What do they expect of him, be a perfect angel?"

GARY: "Which boy you talking about here, Dad?"

EARL: "You know perfectly well which boy. You think I'm talking about that rich snot?"

GARY: "So you think Billy got a raw deal? I'd say we're the ones got a raw deal, all of *us*."

EARL: "Perfectly correct. We're getting screwed. We're getting hammered. No argument from old Earl Hutchins. One hundred percent. Old put-out-to-pasture Earl."

GARY: "But you don't see how Billy caused all this … "

EARL: "*Caused* it? Billy just got mashed up in the gears of it. That's my point. Sure he's involved. He got chewed up in it."

GARY: "You're saying Billy was a victim, too."

EARL: "I'm saying, it was inevitable."

GARY: "Now there, *there*, I would agree with you, Pops. For once I'd agree. Billy gets involved, it's inevitable."

EARL: "Saint William? Ever heard of a Saint William?"

GARY: "You hear me? You listening to me at all?"

EARL: "No Saint William I ever heard of. Everybody casting all these aspersions on him, his own brother included, all I'd point out is at least he tried to do something. Hey, I worked with that little prick every day, every hour. You think that was fun? Well hell yes, if you got a funny idea of fun it was. And I do. That's my point, Gary. I do. All kinds of things make me laugh. Always did. Old Earl, what's with him, gets a laugh out of a bump on a log."

GARY: "How much you had to drink, Earl?"

EARL: "See that's where people go off the rails. They start hearing something they don't want to hear, first thing they say, 'You been drinkin'? You soused as a pickle?'"

GARY: "Just wondering, that's all."

EARL: "*Just wonderin', that's all.*"

GARY: "I don't know how to talk to you, Earl."

EARL: "Then just don't. I'll be on my way. Regrets to the missus, would you? Fucked in a barrel, that's what we are."

GARY: "I'll pass your sympathies along."

EARL: "You haven't seen him, have you?"

GARY: "Billy?"

EARL: "If you got a curse on you, it's not your fault, did I make myself clear on that point?"

GARY: "Oh, that was your point?"

EARL *(mounting Harley)*: "Should've whupped you more."

GARY *(back to work)*: "No, I haven't seen Billy."

On the Island, Three in the Morning

There wasn't a Keysinger around, but the housekeeper, Doris Slater, was staying overnight downstairs and was awakened by a ruckus in the front drive. In a bath of moonlight there was the stark gray outline of a car and Billy Hutchins pissing in the driveway, so uncertain on his feet that he was pissing one way and another, as he shouted, in the full capacity of his lungs, "Hey Rog! You mind if I call you Rog? Your wife's a lousy lay!"

The Showdown

Just as those who have seen great football games in the snow tend to remember these before any others, so the fans of the Derby in Bealport remembered the ones when it rained. The violence, the desperation, the roles of luck and grit, all were magnified in the rain. Cars skidded and slalomed. When there was blood it glistened on steel and mixed with the mud until the event became more a passion play than a sport. And the harder it rained, the louder the fans in the covered grandstand cheered.

On the night that Billy Hutchins' Honda Civic went up against Gary Hutchins' Lincoln, a front was moving in. The weather-dot-com said the rain would start at seven o'clock and it started at a quarter to eight. It rained slantwise, then stopped, then rained slant-wise again, with lightning that lit up the cars so that they looked like Christmas tree ornaments. By the time the powder puff for the ladies had been run, and the pocket rocket for the compacts only, the pit was like running sores. Charlie Russell pulled out of it, and Harv Furman likewise, and Mike Tozier had scratched earlier on account of problems with his differential, so that by the time the main event was due, there were only five entrants left.

Billy took lightly the jeers of the crowd. If he was one of them, he'd be jeering too. This was Billy being either fair-minded or light-headed. He knew he'd screwed up. In a sense, on a reflection that took a few days to mature, it was nothing more than he expected of himself. So he had his big grin for the grandstand, when he drove out to the pit in the little Honda and stood beside it as protocol demanded, rain or shine, mud or dust, for the introduction of the drivers. He tipped his dripping hat as the crowd hooted at him, drowning out his name. A few threw boxes of popcorn and beer cans, but it was too far a throw to reach. Then Gary came out, his Lincoln roaring like a circus lion, amid cheers and cries for blood. The other cars were forgotten. The crowd knew what this was about.

If the brothers exchanged a look, it was hard to tell from the crowd. It was as if neither wished to give the other the satisfaction, Gary's glance wandering over the field of competition, not deigning quite to alight, Billy playing to the hooting crowd. The rain came back harder as they stood there.

The first moves were Pete Hammond's, thinking to take Billy out fast, both because a smaller field early worked to the advantage of Pete's slow-steering old Caprice and because he hated Billy for costing him his job. He came at Billy's flank but Billy skidded away and spun around. Pete came at him again, plowing him backwards off the pit. He had him stalled in the smoking grass and would have finished him head on but Gary came out of what must have been nowhere and rolled him up and over, so that Pete's wheels, still spinning, were like a dog's feet in the air. Pete was done but got out easy and walked away. Gary was saving Billy for himself.

There wasn't a moment when Billy was afraid. He was already a strong believer in the worst that could happen. And if he won, he'd be either happy or he wouldn't be, but it would be a proper kiss good-bye, a kiss to remember him by. He couldn't even remember why he wanted to beat Gary so bad. He fired his engine and came back in the pit. He circled round and round, as if no one could catch him if he made great loops.

Gary knocked Sheldon Coby's Olds to kingdom come with a rear end broadside then went after Ed Markham in his ancient Checker cab. The Checker had taken many poundings down the years and for a big car was agile on its feet, but Ed had played it cheap as he always did and stuck with an old bald set of Royals where the rubber had gone hard as rocks. The mud was worst at the pit's center, where the two of them slopped and slid and fought it out, dinosaur men in dinosaur cars, while Billy flitted around and laughed. It had been five years since Ed took Gary down and it was not to be again. Ed's hard old Royals were helpless in the sea of mud, he was soon a foundering giant, and Gary got enough traction going at a thirty- or thirty-five-degree angle on the Checker's rear flank that he plowed through to the gas tank, which exploded with a bang and a banshee whine as if the lightning itself had hit it. The tank should have been in the back seat but Ed had been too cheap for that too. It was raining so hard by then that the retardant was hardly needed.

Then lightning struck a pole in the deep outfield of the fairgrounds. If it was a sign for anything, it was a sign for a few faint hearts to leave. But even as the rain slashed across the grandstand and the breeze became a gale, most of the Bealporters huddled and drank down what was still in their hands and stayed put for the final attraction.

Now the lightning strikes came so fast that you could say the pit was lit up by the heavens, as Gary and Billy were left with nothing to look at but each other. Strobed by the lightning and blurred by the rain, each waited for the other to make a move. Gary saw the little Honda as defiance and disrespect and an oddly mocking irresponsibility, a middle finger on wheels. Billy saw the Lincoln as a lumbering sad sack, overweight and clinging to power, ripe for the taking.

Billy made the first move, nipping at Gary's wheels, hoping to break an axle. When the probe went nowhere, he fled away, clear out of the pit, up the mound of mud they called The Hill. Gary went after him on The Hill and chased him off.

Now Gary commanded the little height from which maximum acceleration could be had and, throwing into reverse, came rocketing down into a storm of mud as Billy slipped away. Unprotected by windshield or window, momentarily blinded by the waves of mud, Gary could hardly have been more surprised when Billy came around out of the blindness to deliver the cheapest shot of all, a door shot on the driver's side, the sort of blow that will never disable a car but will put its driver in the hospital.

Did Billy know what he was doing? Of course he knew, but he figured he'd never seen Gary in a hospital yet and he'd known him thirty-two years and with his little Honda he would need all the help he could get.

Gary's door cracked and his ribs ached but all Billy really succeeded in doing was teeing him off. He made a squealing turnaround in the mud and came at Billy head on. Which is what you did in the Derby, you started out using your reverse, because that's what sensible tactics demanded, to save your radiator and everything else, to keep you in the game, but then something made you crazy and stupid and you went head on from there.

Billy maneuvered but Gary caught a fender and stove his trunk up, even while knowing you can't kill a front-wheel drive from the rear. He just wanted to make Billy look bad. And he did, he looked ridiculous, like a rooster with its feathers up. But Billy could get mad too. He could be made not to care about bones or blood. He could be made not to care about anything, really, other than that Gary had always been right and Billy had always been wrong. If that was a lie, at least it was his own lie.

In the black soup, in the rain, illuminated as if by Goya, Gary and Billy faced off against each other. It was a contest Billy could not win but felt he could not lose. Gary aimed again at the Civic head on. Billy hardly flinched. The Lincoln's sweeping bumper crashed through the small car's grill and crushed its radiator. Billy braced and shuddered and his forehead hit the wheel. He was showered with mud as well, so that his face coated over with a paste of mud and blood.

Gary could hardly see. He lined up the Civic again. But – was this even possible? – before he could charge the Civic, the Civic was charging him, coming out of the storm like a ghost and the Devil take the rest. The two cars met in what was a no-man's-land now. They crashed, backed off, and crashed again. Billy had only his front end left, there was no car at all in back of the seats, he drove himself forward on his broken front wheels alone. But still he wasn't done. If you move, you're alive.

Somewhere in Bealport, then, a falling tree limb hit a wire and the lone pole of lights at the fairgrounds went black. The crowd went quiet, in uncertainty and waiting, as if it too had had its power cut. Now only the flashes of lightning showed Gary and Billy to each other.

It was Billy who made the one last move. Like an animal that'd lost its hind legs, the Civic willed itself up The Hill, its front wheels grinding and spinning. In the lightning it looked like myth up there and even Gary took note. He wheeled to get out of the way of Billy's crippled charge but the mud spun him around just so and with the last bit of secret steel hidden in his bumper (and without a doubt aided by the momentum of the Lincoln's wrong-way slide), Billy plowed through Gary's passenger-side door and tore the battery on the floor from its strapping and its cables both. Both cars were dead, and both drivers, it seemed briefly, nearly so. The judges in the dark had no choice but to call it a draw. The dampened crowd cheered impartially, as if the rain had washed something away.

On account of the power failure the award ceremony by the chain-link fence was canceled, but on the way down from the grandstand there seemed general agreement that, especially with all the weather and then the outage, it had been one of the better Derbies in a long, long time. Gary and Billy split the five-hundred-dollar prize from Excelsior Sports.

Falling Apart

Gary was hard to hurt but he hurt after the Derby. Over the weekend, Martha tended to him. He sat in the Barcalounger with his hands on the arms of it, palms down, in such a pose as to say that a man's home might really be his castle after all, and she bandaged his face and arms and feet and massaged his neck where the muscles were strained. She had already taped up his ribs with a long roll of Johnson's tape. It wasn't the first time she'd played nurse after a Derby but this time was the worst. Sitting in the grandstand, she'd had moments of praying for his life. Praying for Billy's life, too, as it seemed possible the two meant to kill each other. They, Martha and Gary, were there in the small curtained living room of their fifties tract house when Jerome appeared from upstairs, having nothing more to do of a Saturday evening, unfortunately, than play on the computer. He had a deadpan look, but he often did. "Mom, there's something online. Don't you know this guy, Ravi?"

"Ravi Banerjee?"

"I think so. Isn't he the guy … "

"I don't *know* him."

"Well he's wanted."

She stopped massaging Gary's neck. "What do you mean he's *wanted*?"

"You know, like wanted," Jerome said.

"Like by the police?"

"You want me to show it to you?"

"Are you kidding now? Don't you be kidding me now, Jerome."

"I'm not," Jerome said.

The further details were that Ravi Banerjee, an Indian lecturer and founder of the Spark of Life School in Dearborn, Michigan and a frequent guest on national public television, had last been seen two weeks ago in Little Rock, Arkansas. It was believed that prior to his disappearance on August 3rd, he had withdrawn two hundred fifty-six thousand dollars from a bank account of the Spark of Life Foundation, which had recently been undergoing an Internal Revenue Service review of its tax-exempt status. It was IRS auditors who alerted the police to his disappearance.

Martha had paid not only her deposit but five hundred fifty dollars in addition to Ravi Banerjee, so that she could avoid false hopes yet seek her own spark of life. She looked at Gary as though none of this could be so.

But it was so, and the computer was upstairs to prove it.

Martha held it together as long as Jerome was in the house. She gave him money for pizza to get him gone. Upstairs now, into their bedroom, to which they retreated as if it would be safer there, or they could think better there, she looked at Gary as if to say "what happened?" She had difficulty with words. A few apologies, shaking her head, and something about "the waste," because of course the money would have been spent regardless, whether Ravi Banerjee absconded or not. Gary, awkward at comforting, not knowing quite what parts to touch of a hurting person, finally just wrapped her up in his own hurting arms. It was only a guess on his part, what to do, but that's what he did, because he couldn't stand for her to shake and cry. Martha wasn't known to fall apart. That was part of Gary's problem. He had no experience of Martha this way. Or little experience, anyway, maybe a few times years ago, before life closed her over and formed her. But her tears on his shirt warmed him. He said to her not to worry about the money, because he'd always earned a dollar. And he joked if he'd only knocked Billy a little harder, he could have had that extra two fifty right there.

Martha said, shaking less now, muffled against his chest, "You really ought to go see him, you know."

"Billy?"

"Who's going to be taking care of him?" she said.

"I don't know," Gary said.

"Please. Just will you do it?" she said.

So the next day he did. He went over to where he believed Billy was staying, in the apartment over Ralphie's, but Billy had cleared out. His things were gone, his BMW was gone, all Ralphie knew was that he left.

The Surprise

The Reverend John Quigley spent the hours before the meeting reminding himself of all the things he mustn't say. He was not to say that as soon as the Soviet Union went down, capitalism became merciless again. He was not to say that it had lost all need to put on a pretty face to persuade the world's hearts and minds. Nor would it be prudent for him to observe that money outflanked labor now, because it could move anywhere on earth at the tap of a button while labor was broken up, balkanized, left to compete against itself in a race to the bottom. Nor would he point out that if this were a game, it would be a most unfair one, you would never have a game where the two teams played by such different rules. These were things he had read and believed. But they would make no more sense to the people of Bealport tonight than they would have last year or any other year. They would listen with wilting ears to his droning on, and whatever they said or didn't say aloud, they would still be thinking pretty much what Gary Hutchins already thought back then. In their minds they would call him an organizer, an outside agitator, a communist, a person from away.

Better anyway to talk about what might be done in the here and now. Better to depend, for instance, on the Bermans, the fondly remembered old owners, whom he'd talked into flying up from Florida, whose tickets he'd even offered to pay, though they turned him down and would pay their own fares. They were "comfortable" down in Naples.

The Bermans were late to arrive. The planes were always late into Bangor, as befitted an airport at the end of the line. Quigley sent Tina up to get them, and meanwhile got the meeting going. The first thing he did was apologize, on account of the name of their previous occasion together. *Next Time Let's Be Prepared.* Words like a bitter hangover. Had they gotten prepared? Had he helped them enough to get prepared? No, he felt he had let them down, and he asked their forgiveness, or at least he said he did, making the simplest moves of which he was capable, knowing the words and hoping his feelings matched up.

It was the biggest crowd the church had seen, perhaps except-ing only Mikey Miles' funeral. Or anyway it would be a close call, between the funeral and this night, loss running neck-and-neck. But who was counting, after all? The Reverend Quigley, from the heights of the pulpit? Perhaps he was, roughly speaking, as if seeking some tangible thing, something to weigh or count or measure out in teaspoons, to gain confidence from. Gary Hutchins was out there tonight, in the last row of the pews but at least he was there, a kind of anchor to the evening's hopes. Even Sean and Kristen Byrick were there, talking about selling their boat, although not till the end of summer, as they might as well get one good season from it. Kristen was telling Dot Bowden that much, with a good-natured fatality one might not have expected of Kristen, as if misfortune was in truth the great equalizer it was sometimes advertised to be.

Quigley's earnest-as-he-could-make-it plea for forgiveness elicited a few come-to-Jesus-style shouts of acceptance, also as earnest as the shouters could make them, but these were muffled in the blanket of disquiet that pervaded the room. On to the business at hand, Quigley thought, and even said, grimacing to acknowledge the bareness of the segue, then called on Bart Barnes, the town manager, to provide the governmental perspective. Barnes was a small, slope-nosed, freckled man who hadn't been popular in Bealport over his three-year tenure, both for seeming somewhat aloof and for the varnished baritone of even his everyday speaking voice that sounded like he'd gone to one of those acting schools for TV commercials to perfect. There was also the fact that he came from New Hampshire, which in some kind of unexplained mental jujitsu seemed to a number of Bealporters to be farther away than John Quigley's Michigan. Barnes thought he was bringing decent news. It was true that tax receipts from the factory provided in the neighborhood of forty percent of the Town of Bealport's revenue, but due to the town's wisdom in following Barnes's advice to establish a rainy day fund, the loss of those taxes wouldn't be felt for two years, within which time of course other solutions would be sought twenty-four seven. The majority of his audience thought Barnes was being self-serving the way he said it, as it was obvious he didn't have to remind people that the rainy day fund was his idea, so he got less credit than he felt he deserved and in consequence even as he stood there was in his mind's eye seeing the resumes he would be sending out next week to towns in Wyoming or maybe Florida, places with better prospects and/or weather. A few sprinkles of applause, then a rain of questions. What if the twenty-four-seven efforts yielded nothing? What would get cut, the school, the fire, the roads, everything? What about the new gym for the high school, would that have to be put on hold? Put on hold? What about just plain forgotten? Didn't anyone have any priorities around here? What was the state doing? Had he called up the governor's office?

The town manager provided such answers as he could. The state would be sending its labor relations specialists to liaise with the federal government's Rapid Response Team, in terms of job retraining and the like. It was too soon to talk about cuts, there'd be time enough down the road, if worse came to worst. The people in front of him didn't like his clichés much, but even less they liked the word "liaise." Government gobbledygook. One of those words meant to fool everybody including possibly Bart Barnes himself into thinking something was happening when nothing was. Peg Eaton "whispered," loud enough to be heard several pews away, that it sounded like something that was supposed to happen between the sheets.

Next up was Miss Nell Wheaton, from a prominent shoe store in Portland, where, as was said when she was introduced, they still had a couple of shoe stores as opposed to "shoe outlets" or "shoes for less." Like a manager bringing in a lefty to pitch to one batter only, Quigley had recruited her for one line: Norumbega shoes were selling in Portland! But Miss Wheaton, a trim woman with feisty hair who was even a bit shorter than she looked, hadn't driven all the way from Portland to deliver one line. She wanted these wonderful Maine workers to know that her customers *loved* Norumbega shoes, they loved the new line of bucks, they loved the old loafers, the businessmen were going for the cordovans, and even in the last few days, as soon as word of the closing hit the paper, there were people coming in and buying extra pairs, "stocking up" as it were.

Meanwhile the Reverend Quigley flicked glances at his watch and wondered where the Bermans were. The Bermans were his hole card, his surprise, the planned climax to his carefully choreographed evening. Not that he wasn't grateful for Nell Wheaton. She fired up the beleaguered home team. She confirmed what they longed to hear. And she was the perfect setup for Quigley himself.

For what Quigley had to say was that Norumbega was a profitable business, and profitable businesses don't just go away. That was a matter not of faith but of fact. They only had to find a buyer! And how could there not be a buyer, somewhere, for the maker of a beautiful product, a useful product, for pity's sake a *profitable* product, that was catching on, that was in more stores every month, that people with money wanted to buy? For wasn't that the secret truth: these days there were people with money and people with no money, and if you wanted to have money yourself, you had to have something that the people with the money wanted. And they did, they had a hit on their hands, just check the sales figures, just listen to Miss Nell Wheaton.

It was probably the best sermon the Reverend John Quigley ever delivered, the most rousing anyway, the one where he came closest to getting his heart and his anger in, but all the while he wondered where the Bermans were. Because he had already told everybody: he had a surprise for them tonight. Not a buyer, but anyway a special surprise, that would lift their spirits and give them good advice on what steps to take next, on where to find what they needed. By then his sermon, if that's what it really was, had begun to circle around itself, or anyway he sensed the chance of it, and of a spiral down, so he opened the floor to discussion.

In this stall for time, the people of Bealport were more than obliging. They seemed roused, even, to hope. One after another stood up to describe things they'd seen online, a favorable review here, a prestigious shop there. Others had even more incidental reports, of, say, a cousin in Albany, New York who bought a pair of the loafers and was wearing them every day. If you added everything up that was said, it would perhaps have made only a small bundle. But those in the church on this evening didn't seem to notice how small it was. Perhaps in the morning they would. In the meantime, the Bermans arrived, two small, fragile people in bright Floridian clothes, Mrs. Berman in a wheelchair pushed by Tina Barnes, Hal Berman carrying his wife's white linen jacket on his arm.

It was a surprise well sprung. John Quigley had no need to say a word. The only thing missing was the music or you might have thought it was a wedding coming down the center aisle. People turned, the way people do, on those occasions when to gape is not a social sin. Quigley gave the signal to the rest that they should not be afraid to clap. In the middle of applause, he greeted Hal with a happy embrace and bent to kiss Hildy on the cheek.

The troubled expression on Hal Berman's face might have been read as puzzlement as to what all the fuss was about. Quigley would not have seen it anyway, as he was addressing the assembled again, reminding them of the nineteen years that the Bermans had successfully steered Norumbega and of Hal Berman's wide-ranging expertise in the shoe business. Perhaps it was the flattery that troubled Berman, Martha Hutchins thought, as she could remember he was a modest man with a tendency even to blush when no one else in the world would think to bat an eye. Quigley continued: "I asked Hal and Hildy, whom you know I never met personally before, but a few days ago I called them, sort of out of the blue, and explained who I was, and asked if they'd lend their experience and advice to give us a hand at this difficult moment. They didn't hesitate a second. Hal said he'd get right to work, analyze the firm's financials, send out feelers to potential buyers. And he said they'd be here when we needed them. And here they are tonight … What can you tell us, Hal?"

But before a second round of applause could start, Hal Berman shook his head. It seemed he didn't want the applause. He said something that couldn't be heard, though it's possible John Quigley heard it, as he was standing close by. Regardless, he handed old Mr. Berman the mike. Now the sandy voice of uncertain pitch could be heard, as Hal Berman pronounced, with sadness, "Not good news."

If the Reverend Quigley had trained as a lawyer, he would have known never to ask a question that he didn't know the answer to. But he was not trained as a lawyer. Behind his wire-rimmed glasses, his eyes shrunk and hardened, as if they'd been embalmed for a diorama of distress. "Oh?" he said.

"The problem is," Berman said, "you got a good product, good workers, good sales … but the company's loaded up with debt. Who's going to buy a company that's leveraged up to its armpits? The current owners took all the money out of it. Bank loans, more bank loans. They must have paid themselves off big."

All the lift went out of Quigley's voice. "Can they do that?"

"Can they do that? They do it all the time. That's what these guys do. They buy companies and that's what they do," Berman said.

Quigley ran out of questions. It felt as if his memory, of even where he was, was wiped clean.

To fill the void, being a man who was afraid he might be blamed for any voids, even those, for instance, that might pop up anywhere in the universe, Berman said, "I'm sorry to be the one who had to tell you."

"Please don't kill the messenger," Hildy Berman said, but because she had no mike and her voice was even paler than her husband's, it was unclear if anybody heard.

The Continuing Life and Times of Wsbealport1

Wsbealport1, a.k.a. Burton Miles, had a fair estimation of the likely financial resources of his fellow Winter Soldiers, but at the same time he felt that in an online situation you could never know for sure about who you were in actual communication with or not. So he posted in the chat room the following: "Anybody knows a comrade with a few million in spare currency who might want to put it in a profitable business to support American jobs, don't be shy about getting in contact."

His posting did not go overlooked. *Wsfrankr* commiserated. No, he didn't have any billionaires living next door, but he did believe in the power of the American working man and eventually quality would win out, always had and always will. *Wsfrankr* took his share of mockery and disbelief for that one. *Wsstormboy* meanwhile got back to his old thought of getting Mikey Miles nominated as a martyr to the cause. He apologized to *wsbealport1* for allowing this whole thing to slide, but he could see now clearer than ever that what Mikey was fighting was bigger than all of them. *Wslancaster3* said amen to that one. *Wsformerfratboy* criticized the others for once again straying from the topic at hand, which in this case was did any of them know any billionaires. But none of them did, or at least if they did, none of them cared to reveal their source. *Wsbigtime88* mentioned Bill Gates, but he couldn't lay claim to knowing him personally. *Wsnorwalk1*, in a similar vein, said the Rockefellers should be checked out. *Wsstormboy*, not to be deterred by the likes of *wsformerfratboy*, reposted an old photo of Mikey Miles in his hunting outfit that Burton had previously shared, and suggested that every single Winter Soldier would do well to have it on their desktops and use it in their posts. *Wsfarmingdale, wsgeorgewashingtonbridge, wsnathanhale14,* and *wspeapodonthecape* all posted the photo at once. *Wsbealport1* thanked them all for their sympathy and sensitivity and said his son Mikey would be proud to be so honored by them, but expressed some degree of doubt as to whether it would help bring his shoe factory back. *Wsstormboy* observed that you had to start somewhere. And who could argue with that?

A Secret

The equivalent might have been seeing his father go into a whore-house. From the internet Jerome had a fairly accurate idea of what a whorehouse was, even if he was very far from having ever visited such a place himself or even knowing where one was. He imagined there might be one in Bangor, Bangor being Jerome's idea of a city. Or over in Brewer, maybe upstairs from or next door to the place that said XXX ADULT MOVIES LIVE MODELS XXX across the whole front window so that you could see nothing at all of what went on inside. Jerome's neck had stiffened a few times as he tried to catch glimpses of the place as they drove by. But, anyway, it wasn't that. Seeing your father go into a whorehouse was something from a movie he'd seen. What happened instead was this: Jerome, being a bit finicky regarding his computer, always checked his trash before deleting it, in case something got in there that shouldn't have. On one such occasion, he saw the note Gary wrote to Rog Keysinger. Gary had known enough about the computer to trash the note after he printed it, but not enough to delete the trash. So there it was for Jerome to open, out of nothing more than curiosity as to what his father had been just a little furtive about: "Dear Mr. Keysinger."

The way they say "too much information," it was way too much for Jerome. Uncle Billy having been fired, not two weeks ago, but years ago, for drug dealing. His own father being the squealer. Wasn't that what they called people like that, everywhere you read, every-thing you were told? "Squealer" was the old standby but what about the sneak, the snitch, the rat? His father was a rat. Jerome's mind kept saying *squealer*, even if it was old-fashioned, because, somehow, being so old fashioned, it didn't sound quite as bad as the others.

It was the truth, but not quite as bad a truth. "Rat," too, was old fashioned, but a rat, possibly, should be killed, whereas a squealer might only be beaten.

It was his father, then, that got the plant shut down. What other conclusion could Jerome draw? His father sent the secret letter that alerted Mr. Keysinger to Billy and then Billy was fired and the plant shut down. The logic of it felt like a helmet, squeezing Jerome's brain, inevitable, inescapable. Every time he tried to think of something else, in two seconds, it seemed, he was back to this. His father was not who he thought he was. His father was a squealer. His father had a secret and now Jerome had it too.

Everyone was wondering about Jerome, but he wouldn't say. It was bad enough that he knew the truth, so how much worse would it be if it got out? And how much infinitely worse than that if it came out on account of him? He felt stronger than his father. He felt his father needed his protection, even if the protection was only from Gary himself. He must not waver. When he looked at his father now, he saw blubber, he saw weakness, so he tried not to look at him at all. Even at dinner, he ate quickly and answered questions in a kind of shorthand so abbreviated that it sometimes made no sense, and then he left.

His mother speculated that he might be in love, but that was Martha looking to the upside of things, after so many waves of bad news. She acknowledged it could also be the plant closing. Gary said it could be that, and there'd been counselors sent to the schools to talk about what might now happen, to reassure, and maybe to lie. Gary tried to broach that very subject with Jerome, to tell him that the house was mostly paid up and that his mother and himself would find work, because they always did and it wasn't the end of the world.

Jerome listened with only half his ears. Over the days he began to see only one way out. He could tell his father that he knew. At least, then, there could be two people in on the same secret. But he was afraid his father would hate him then, for knowing, for telling, for disbelieving. Because wasn't that he was doing, disbelieving in his father? A stupid computer file says this about your father and you believe it? And yet he did. Computers don't lie, don't make up words, they only do what you tell them to do. That was one thing Jerome could still believe.

Jerome decided to go out to the garage and have a talk with him. In the end, it seemed like the manly thing. He felt six feet tall then – that is to say, for a change, exactly as tall as he was. He would get out such words as were necessary, blurt them if necessary, even if he was shaking as he shook now, with his hands stiff in his pockets to hold the shaking down, walking from the back porch to the garage where even though it wasn't quite dark, the lights were already on. Burning a hole in daylight, as they say, or in this case, the twilight. Jerome had always loved going in his dad's garage. It smelled of Gary, of getting things done.

The Lincoln was more bent up than it had ever been. Gary was saying it would take him pretty much the whole year to get it back where it was. That was to Jerome he was speaking, who hadn't been in the garage for awhile, so that Gary took it as a good sign and talked to him the way he always did when the two of them were out there, about the mechanics of things.

Gary kept working. He was halfway under the car. Jerome watched him with disbelieving eyes. "Looks good," Jerome said, finding those two words alone in his dry mouth.

"You've got to be kidding," Gary said. "Looks like a total piece of shit to me."

Gary was comforted to get some swear words out. It made it seem like things were all right between himself and his son. In a sense, it declared that they were. The garage had always been the place where Gary felt free to tell his son how things really were.

And Jerome knew this. He wanted to laugh, because things seemed like they'd always been. It was a relief to be in a place where everything contradicted what he knew, where the past still prevailed. But he couldn't laugh. The illusion wasn't strong enough. The patheticness of his father, on the ground, half under the car, not even knowing who had discovered his secret, unnerved him. If his father caused the whole town of Bealport to lose everything, why wasn't he showing it? His father must be a monster.

Jerome tried again to talk to *this person*. "So Dad … "

"What? You start to say something?"

But Jerome's words lost their way. If he lied, if he told the truth, if he said something, if he said nothing: Jerome could see all the possibilities. None of them was any better. He was sorry he walked in. Everything was worse now.

"Yes, yeah, I do. I'm uh … I've been thinking … I'm going to go to Hancock."

Gary put his wrench down, though he wasn't really surprised. The only thing that surprised him was that this was what had been on Jerome's mind. And it was a relief, really. Going to Hancock. Well, why not. Gary, as he stopped to think about it, had had a change of heart on the subject. Bealport was going to hell, anyway. That was the difference. He could see that now.

"It have to do with the factory closing, son?"

"No, I've been thinking about it awhile," Jerome said.

"Can't say I blame you," Gary said, and picked up his wrench again. He was playacting somewhat when he did that, to hide his emotion, but it wasn't all playacting.

Whether Jerome had been thinking about it before he said it, even he couldn't say. Of course it wasn't what he meant to say. But he couldn't say what he meant to. Nor could he even think to himself that the reason most of all to go to Hancock Latin was that his father wasn't who he thought. Jerome would go back to his secret and hide it forever and that would be better. He hadn't lived long enough to forget things yet, but he had the idea of forgetting, and one day it might happen. His mother was pleased with his decision regarding schools.

The Tower

The old saw about there being no atheists in a foxhole: the Reverend John Quigley thought about it anyway. He resented certain of its implications, its sorry critique of man's ambitions in the spiritual domain for one thing, its singling out foxholes as so special against the whole wide world of suffering for another. But perhaps there was as much truth in it as in that other whiskered old thing you heard, nothing concentrates the mind like a hanging in the morning. The morning wasn't far off now. So the Reverend Quigley found himself praying again. He prayed in his study, in his car on the way to work, and in his house when Tina wasn't around. He didn't want her to see him on his knees. He didn't want to hurt her feelings, by suggesting a kind of superiority. She was tender enough as is. He would lead her to God in other ways. He was praying for guidance and felt like a phony every word and thought and breath of the way.

Then he bowed to the inevitable. On the second Sunday after the community meeting where the Bermans appeared and diminished his hopes, Quigley, in place of his customary sermon, broached to his congregation the subject he had long avoided. It was a much smaller crowd in front of him than appeared on the night of the meeting. Perhaps seventy-odd parishioners, and if you wanted to do a head count, what you would see was a field of gray and white and bald. The regulars, really. The people who came from a habit of piety, though you might have left off the last two words and been just as close to the fact. Who could say for sure, who was the king of hearts? Quigley reminded his flock of their new hymnals. He advised them not to open them to a hymn but rather to the inside back covers, and to see the little stickers there. "I mentioned these people some months ago. Maybe you remember, our friends at Aspirational Technology?"

A few murmurs of "I do" from the congregation, who were used to answering the questions, even the rhetorical ones, as if no one would be so silly as to ask a question they didn't want the answer to.

Quigley said: "Well, anyway, let me be frank, my friends. They *bribed* me. I didn't mention it at the time, I didn't want to stir up anybody getting excited, but it was a *bribe.* I took it because we could use the new hymnals, as you know the old ones were in sorry shape. So I thought to myself then: I'll take the new ones, because really they came with no strings attached. But there *was* one little string – every time I look at one of these books, frankly, I remember what Aspirational Technology wants me to remember. They want to take our church steeple, that's been around almost as long as our country's been around, and put a cell phone tower inside it. And in return for that, they'd pay us some pretty good money, money that would go a ways to paying some of our bills and keeping our building, the steeple itself, the whole place, in shape.

"In exchange, there'd be this big steel thing, with a lot of power used to supply it, directly above us, and also possibly emitting some humming noises or whatever, or maybe not, or maybe other problems, but maybe not. A lot of churches across the country have gone for this. So you can see, I'm not trying to prejudice the case one way or the other.

"But what I thought back then was: we don't need this, because Bealport had just been saved. I know you'll know what I'm referring to here. If the town has jobs, if there's a business that's always been contributing to the jobs, keeping a bit of money in everybody's pockets, then we don't need Aspirational Technology. Let's not start getting greedy, I thought.

"Well I don't have to tell any of you what's changed. So here we are today and I can't tell you what to do, especially about a steeple that's been around for two hundred years and I've only been around three years, but I felt we ought to open it to discussion. I want your guidance, your thoughts. And we don't have to decide anything today. I'll put the plans in the parish room and you can see what they're talking about. And anybody wants to go online, there's a lot of churches out there to report their experiences."

"Will you see it?" Dot Bowden wanted to know.

"Not according to what they say," Quigley said.

"Not even the extension cords?" Dot was a persistent one.

"I'm not sure, Dot, but I doubt they use extension cords."

"Well what do they use then?"

"Actually, I'm not sure."

"In my own house, even, I hate the sight of an unsightly extension cord. Running all over the place. That's one thing I wouldn't want."

"I'll look into that, Dot, okay?"

Dot folded her arms and whispered something to Maggie Winslow beside her, and that was the end of the extension cord discussion.

Fox Herman then wanted to know if the anticipated funds from the tower would be going to pay a part of the pastor's own salary, and if that was influencing his decision or not. Fox was taking his customarily aggressive tone, wanting to make sure no fast ones were being pulled.

"Fox, I don't think I can answer that question," Quigley replied. "Because we've got a general fund, right? So if money comes in, it gets mixed with the rest. We'd be hard put to say what was going for what. But more important: I don't have a decision to make on this. I'm putting it up to all of you."

Tim Raines, the local cab driver, of Tim's Taxi, said he understood the Reverend was putting it out there for them, but still, if he, the Reverend, had to make the decision, if it was up to him, what would he do?

Quigley pushed his glasses up and thought a moment, or at least gave the impression of thinking, as he wanted all to know this would be no easy call. "I suppose, as of today, I'd say probably we should think of doing it. I don't see any other saviors on the horizon."

Which may have been an unfortunate way to put it, as it left the opening for Charlie Russell and one or two others, more or less simultaneously, to mutter "What about God?" or words to that effect, and cause a stir in their pews.

From there, Peg Eaton wanted to know the terms of the lease, how many years and so on and if the company didn't live up to its side of whatever the bargain was, could it be kicked out beforehand? Quigley said absolutely and they'd check with a lawyer before signing anything. Dot Bowden asked about cancer-causing electronic radiation, like you read about coming from the power poles. Quigley said he believed there were studies that showed none of that happening. Dot said you can't believe those studies. Furthermore she happened to know of two people over in South China Lake, living in the same house, who were both killed with cancer from the power poles. She repeated that you can't believe all these studies, one thing says one, the other says the other. Morris Landrum, a relative newcomer to Bealport, supported the idea of more online investigation of what the experience of others was. Fox Herman said in fact he'd done exactly that investigation, months ago, as soon as he saw those stickers in the hymnals, and what he found was, a., most congregations were okay with it, with few complaints, b., Aspirational Technology got three and a half stars from somewhere but he didn't remember the name of the website.

There were moments that could give the one royalist in the crowd, Zack Tilghman, who was only a royalist because no one else was, some ammunition. The people deciding their own fate, really? Sherry Landrum worried that the parking situation might be affected. Nobody at all understood that one, nor, when asked, could Sherry really explain. Mary Francis Donnelson, regarding what Fox had said about three and a half stars for Aspirational Technology, replied that a lot of those things online were rigged. And how many of those congregations had two hundred year-old steeples, Timmy Thomson wanted to know. If you were out in Arizona with one of those things that looked like Cape Canaveral for a steeple, why, sure, why not have a cell phone tower in it, you would hardly tell the difference, what was which. Mention of Arizona made Ed Parsons inevitably think of Roswell, New Mexico, and everything that entailed, and while he was by no means claiming with certainty that there had been extraterrestrial communication there, still you couldn't dismiss outright the chance that radiation emitted from cell phone transmission might attract attention from deep space. People snickered at Ed, behind his back, as they always did. Several people asked how much money exactly they could expect to get, not seeming to notice that somebody five minutes before had already asked the question and had got the answer from Reverend Quigley that it would have to be negotiated. But the largest number of comments followed along the lines of what Pamela Harrelton said. Pamela was not known to talk much, at church, at the McDonald's, or otherwise. She lived alone with her cats, after her seaman husband failed to return one year from Valparaiso. With honest tears in her eyes, she said she couldn't just sit there with all the comments she was hearing. Didn't people realize what they had? It was like a blessing, to be handed down this beautiful tower, how could they even think of doing anything else but just leaving it be and passing it along? It wasn't about to fall down. So what if they had no money, the people who built it back then for sure had even less, but they climbed up there and built it. Pamela had the kind of passion that drove her to say everything she could, then stop without saying one word more. All she could do was shake her head, with her wet eyes shut, when she was done.

That was the moment John Quigley knew he had a congregation at last. With all their losses, he'd been sure they were going to vote for the money. He would have himself. He would have gone along, the way an ironist will often go along, saving his heart for rearguard actions. But Pamela Harrelton turned it. People seemed to look up. Even he had that urge, to see what was above his head, to know exactly how tall, measured by that same ironic heart, their steeple was. Some of the comments that followed Pamela's were just as silly as those that preceded it. But even the silly ones had a vector. Marcie Phelps thought they might raise money, in place of what the cell phone people were offering, by having a contest where people guessed, down to the inch, how tall the tower was, and if anybody got it down to one inch or less, they won. Fox Herman, chuckling in his fashion, asked Marcie why not offer sky dive rides off the steeple while they were at it. Peg Eaton said what they should really be doing was getting the whole church on the national registry of historic places. Standish Brown said that might only bring a lot of federal regulation, like they could stop you from even planting a bush in front. Deb Francis wanted to know, if they decided to turn the cell phone people down, if they would have to send the hymnals back. Then, when the Reverend Quigley said no, she asked whether in good conscience they should. Frank Benn said how could they send them back, they were already used, he'd reliably seen dried snot inside one of them. It went on like that, until almost twelve-thirty, well past the Sunday dinner hour. Tired, hungry, and with prayers still to offer, benedictions still to receive and hymns still to sing from the bright red *Pilgrim Hymnals* that even now smelled inky fresh, the parishioners of the First Congregational Church of Bealport, after voting unanimously that they needed no more time to decide, further voted sixty-four to eleven to keep the steeple the way it was.

Five days later, on the first of September, as previously announced, the factory closed.

The New Idea

One of the best jobs left for a person like Martha Hutchins was cleaning houses. For one thing, she liked to clean. She'd always been pretty good at it. And down to the Island they were paying eighteen dollars an hour for housecleaning, because of the overall shortage of people interested in doing that sort of work and because, the way it seemed, there were every year more people on the Island with more money who wanted more housecleaning. Not many on the Island did it themselves. There were some these days who had their houses cleaned five days a week. Martha felt that was excessive, except possibly if you had an extremely large house, but who was she to complain? "The more work, the merrier" would definitely be overstating the case. But at least they weren't on food stamps yet. When Martha was young, her family had received the government cheese for awhile. Even if it was regular American cheese the only difference being that the government passed it out, Martha never wanted to eat government cheese again.

She cleaned house for the Coffmans of Rye, New York, the Brehlings of West Hartford, Connecticut, the Williamses of Baltimore, the Peachtrees of Lake Forest, Illinois, and the Smiths of Newton, Massachusetts, but not for the Keysingers. The Keysingers were either well provided for in the housecleaning area or they had an embargo going on the last name Hutchins. Martha didn't really care which one it was. She had enough to do. Though the rumor had it that the Keysingers had done some housecleaning themselves and fired everybody who had anything to do with Matt Farnsworth. The recently arrested Matt Farnsworth, it could be added, though whether the sheriff had a real case against him or it was just a nuisance bust instigated by the Keysingers had been a matter for morning discussion at the McDonald's. Meanwhile, five days a week, Martha scrubbed floors, sanitized toilets, washed windows to a state of near invisibility, dusted, vacuumed, swept, and Pledged. This continued even into October and November. They wanted their places kept up even when they were gone for the season. It wasn't like the old days on the Island, when people just locked the door, drained the pipes, and went home. Every day, after work, Martha counted up whether she had yet repaid the seven hundred fifty dollars she lost to the Indian who had such a wonderful idea and manner.

Gary had long sworn that he would never do the work that was the obvious parallel to Martha's, namely, caretaking. Caretaking, in his view, lacked dignity. Or possibly it had dignity, if you allowed as all work had an amount of dignity, but it was too personal, you had to put up with too much of the personal garbage of the rich. Moreover it was work not as readily available as cleaning houses, in that people tended to keep their caretaker over a number of years. But the elimination, temporary or otherwise, of Matt Farnsworth from the profession created an opportunity that Gary, otherwise sitting by the television or making too fast progress on his Lincoln, found himself hard pressed to explain to Martha why he should ignore. So even if the Keysingers had established an employment embargo against all Hutchinses, there were still Matt's other clients to pursue, and Gary, with his reputation for dependability and overall competence, soon had the Macons, the Bernsteins, and the Donaldsons lined up.

But Gary was unhappy. He was unhappier than Martha at this point. And, unlike her, he kept looking for a way out. This couldn't be the way things were now going to be. He refused. "I'll kill myself," that sort of thing, but they were empty words. He was probably the least likely person to kill himself in the whole county, and he knew it. It was just that the unfairness of life was registering on him, perhaps not as a fact, but at least as a strong possibility, one where the dial was in the red. Then one morning that unfairness disappeared, so completely that Gary could remember hardly a thing about it, what it felt like, smelled or tasted like, the weight of it in his shoulders, even how it was correctly spelled in his mind's dictionary. Gary had an idea.

He waited for other mornings to flesh it out before telling Martha. It was their arrangement for him to pick her up after work in the truck. The truck, on the few miles from the Island back to town, was where they had taken to saying anything new or halfway controversial to each other. It kept Jerome out of the loop. They could tell him what they'd decided later. As they approached the rickety bridge that had survived another season, as if all the complaints and inaction had only served to fortify its stubbornness, Gary told her what he'd been thinking about.

And he slowed down, because he knew Martha was more receptive to his ideas when he wasn't driving fast.

GARY: "Okay, so what do you think of this one? I've been thinking about this all week. So it was sort of Billy's idea. I admit that. But he didn't follow it through, as usual. I never said he didn't have ideas. He's my brother, he couldn't be a total idiot … "

MARTHA: "Gary … "

GARY: "What?"

MARTHA: "What is it? What's the idea?"

GARY: "I'm getting to it. Just let me get to it. I just want you to know, so you don't think I'm stealing something from Billy."

MARTHA: "Why would I think that?"

GARY: "All right. Okay. This is it, then. What about … we don't just make expensive shoes. That's the right direction, but we take it one step off the bridge. We go all the way. We make *custom* shoes. The guy flies in on his private jet, okay, he comes to Bealport, we take his measurements, make the lasts, and from then on, whatever he wants, leathers, styles, we make it. A thousand dollars a pair! Maybe more, two thousand!

MARTHA: "You really think people would fly up here on their private jet for a pair of shoes?"

GARY: "Or I don't know. Who knows? Or if they didn't want to, they could send the jet, we could fly down. I could fly."

MARTHA: "Gary, you've never been on a plane in your life."

GARY: "That's ridiculous. I just didn't need to. You tell me when I needed to fly on a plane."

MARTHA: "It's a sweet idea, really."

GARY: "Sweet? *Sweet?* For God's sake! Okay, okay, forget the plane. We don't even need the plane. What about, just the people on the Island? You think Tom Bernstein couldn't afford two thousand dollars for a pair of shoes? Of course he could. Mr. Donaldson just the same."

MARTHA: "I don't know, Gary."

GARY: "Hey, I don't know either. Who knows? But it's an idea, anyway. You've got to have an idea. We could use the internet."

MARTHA: "The internet?"

GARY: "Get the word out. Best American shoemakers around. Custom made."

MARTHA: "Don't people go to England if they want custom shoes, if they've got all that money?"

GARY: "That's it! Don't you see? We just got to persuade 'em that we're even better."

MARTHA: "Like Cadillac's better than Mercedes-Benz? I don't know."

GARY: "What do you know about Mercedes-Benz?"

MARTHA: "Enough."

GARY: "Jesus, Martha. Couldn't you show just a little bit of enthusiasm?"

But she was showing the enthusiasm she could. It wasn't a week ago that she'd been watching the E! channel and there was something on about a new movie where a transvestite saves a shoe company by getting them to make boots for transvestites. Martha didn't imagine there were enough transvestites to save a company like Norumbega, especially as it was also in the article that a place over in England was already doing just that, making boots for transvestites, but wasn't that something? Wasn't it an idea? Wasn't it more of an idea than Gary's? So she showed her enthusiasm by not even telling him what she'd seen. Only Gary couldn't see what she was showing him by not showing him. It was the old thing about how hard it is to prove a negative.

MARTHA (*because it seemed less painful, or perhaps just more relevant, to say this than the other*): "Don't you need money to start a business like that?"

GARY: "We'd have to start small."

MARTHA: "But how small?"

GARY: "I don't know, okay?"

MARTHA: "I'm just trying to be realistic. Like, you don't even know how to make a pair of shoes. All by yourself? Like they used to? Before there were factories?"

GARY: "I'd have to learn. That's all."

MARTHA: "That's *all*?"

GARY: "That's all."

They were quiet the rest of the way. Martha kept thinking of the transvestite in the movie. She would have liked to see that transvestite. And wasn't life passing them by, speeding along, right by them? It wasn't a movie likely to play in Bangor. It saddened her, really. Gary was grumpy and thought, really, of nothing, except maybe that she was a hard one to please.

Certain Things Earl Hutchins Did in the Aftermath of the Closing of Norumbega Footwear

Take his Social Security early. It was true that by taking his Social Security benefit at age sixty-three as opposed to sixty-six, Earl was sacrificing a percentage of what he might have received later. But Earl didn't figure he was going to necessarily live to age sixty-six, and he felt damned if he was going to pay in to the government all those years and get nothing back. Combined with the unemployment benefits for however many weeks they were going to last, the Social Security looked sufficient to pay for repairs to his Harley, liquor, and a modicum of heat in the winter. These were his basic needs, as he saw it. Though of course he would then remember food. Earl was not as averse as some to accepting the food stamps. These would help with the occasional trip to the Hannaford. Overall, Earl was not too worried. He felt, regarding himself personally, that he was not a good candidate for job retraining, even if it wasn't all a crock anyway, which he believed it was.

Transfer his shoemaking skills to his son Gary. Gary came to him and asked him. Earl was flattered, to an extent. On the one hand, he never doubted that he had certain skills which others of for example the next generation could benefit from and were letting go to waste. On the other hand, he had long felt that his son Gary was one of those who were overlooking what they had here, and for Gary to do this about-face was very gratifying. Cut by hand, stretch by hand, stitch by hand, glue and nail by hand, Earl had learned such things from old Uncle Clark Hutchins, who had learned them from so-and-so, who had learned them from so-and-so. Useless knowledge, according to almost everybody, in an age, or even a past age, when you'd do better to learn how to make and use the machines. But Gary wanted to know, so there were nights and weeks, mostly out at the camp, when Earl got out his old shoemaking tools, his awls and hafts, his clicker and scrap hatchet, his nippers, pincers, and shears, that were all wrapped up in an old chamois cloth, and brought out as well a fifth of Jack for a bit of lubrication, and taught Gary "everything he knew." "Everything he knew" was both a lot and a little. Gary already knew about shoes. What he didn't know entirely was what his eyes and his hands could do together, with the help only of this little chamois cloth's worth of instruments. His eyes and hands: Gary came to think of them working together like those ice duets at the Olympics that Martha liked so much to coo about, every four years but it seemed more often than that. Earl was aware, from the outset of those weeks and nights, of Gary's cockamamie idea of making custom shoes for all the big shots who would fly up on their private planes. Earl, never more a realist than when he'd had a few, was gratified, towards the end of their nights together, when Gary confided that he'd put the idea on the shelf, at least for the foreseeable future, in favor of going into the shoe repair business. There was not a shoe repair in twenty miles of Bealport. Even in Bangor there was only one, and if you took your shoes there you had a three-month wait to get them back, that's how busy they were. Earl approved of Gary's recalibration. So did Martha. And with the factory closing, there were soon several storefronts available on Main Street for almost any rent anybody would pay.

Tell Gary he loved him. It was one of those moments you could decide was either mawkish or just awkward, depending on your taste. In Earl's own mind, it was slightly ridiculous, but he'd seen those scenes so often on the television that they had kind of imprinted themselves on his mind. Was that what people really did? Well if it was, then Earl found no reason why he shouldn't too. And he didn't just tell him. He told him he loved him and he loved him just as much as he loved Billy. And he gave him his shoemaking tools wrapped up in the chamois cloth. So there. That was that. He was pretty much sober, too, when he did it, so the booze couldn't get the blame for that one. As for Billy, Earl figured he'd show up again one of these days. If he came back once, he'd probably come back twice, though who could say when.

Tiles

Roger Keysinger was past his infatuation with shoes. The shortest chapter of all, or close. And how predictable? Slightly, fairly, extremely? It would probably depend on your overall outlook which adverb to choose, or whether to choose any adverb at all. Rog was interested in handcrafted Spanish tiles now, those beautiful ones they made in New Mexico. There was a factory north of Albuquerque for sale. Rog felt the possibility that many more Americans than had thus far done so would put them in their gardens. Americans, Canadians, perhaps even Scandinavians, if the price could be made competitive. Keysinger's interest in the tile factory corresponded to the interest he had taken in Marla Dominguez, the woman in her forties with the dark wave of hair and Mediterranean eyebrows whom he had met at The Century Ahead conference. Marla was enamored of handmade tiles herself, and could imagine many innovative designs that could make a tile factory distinctive and fashionable. Rog had entered into negotiations to buy Ceramica Tile of Rio Rancho, New Mexico. He was not interested in divorcing Courtney, on account of the kids and all of that, but he had taken to calling her the ball-and-chain when joking around with his partners in Greenwich, who were giving Rog a freer hand in his negotiations in New Mexico, on account of the money they all made on the shoe factory in Maine.

The Breakfast Hour at the McDonald's

Somebody had to put things in perspective and it was Peggy Eaton who stepped into the role, which in her signature version of it seemed once again to require equal, offsetting parts of hope and scolding. The town had been going through ups and downs from before any of them could remember. People moving, businesses closing. There was no point in everything always staying the same, nor wasting your breath to hope for it. Peg's stoicism elicited from Timmy Thomson an accounting of what had been lost to date, Carl Esposito and his family to Augusta, Tom Lacques to Bangor, the Dinsmores to Orrington, all those others with plans to leave if they could only get a buyer for their house. Con Bowden cut in with a sarcastic laugh there: what was going to keep the town going was that nobody could sell. Timmy resumed counting off with his fingers: Fred's Small Engine, the flower shop, the tanning salon, even the Rite Aid, from what he was hearing, as soon as its lease was up. The average age of the population was bound to go up, that was another factor to consider, Charlie Russell chimed in.

Dawn Smith stared at the floor, which is what she would do when she was trying to think something through and ignore what the others were saying. The result was that when she did speak it was often apropos of nothing, or at least apropos of nothing readily discernible, but the others were used to this from Dawn, she was the kind of person who would say "not to change the subject" when she meant to change the subject. Today she said: "You know I keep thinking, however things turn out, they could be a lot worse. I mean look at all the people worse off than us. The world's actually getting better." "What's your point here exactly, Dawn?" Marge Deschamps asked. It was almost a profession for Marge to go after things Dawn said that didn't appear to make a hundred percent sense. Dawn said: "Well, look at the people in China. The way my mother always made me clean my plate, she said 'think of all the starving people in China.' Isn't that sort of funny? I mean, *now?*" "I wouldn't exactly call it funny," Fox Herman said. "I just think it's weird, that my mother always said that," Dawn said. "Mine too," Cathy Maitland said, trying to help the besieged Dawn out a little. "So there's millions of people in the world not starving who used to. That's *better*, isn't it? Isn't it?" Dawn asked.

It was enough to quiet down the small morning gathering. The crowd at the McDonald's was sometimes smaller than it used to be, on account on variations in how the Rapid Response Team organized the job retraining hours, but also sometimes larger, on account of so many people having less to do most of the day. It was notable that Stump Watkins, the franchise holder, had taken a survey of his customer traffic. What he found was that if you counted all the hours the store was open, he had more daily visits than ever, but with no increase in revenue. Stump attributed this to people hanging out more, buying less, ordering the dollar menu. For a dollar in the morning, you could get a Sausage McMuffin without the egg. The sullen silence of the crowd following Dawn's discovery of a better world was the perfect atmosphere for Burton Miles to spring the great surprise that he'd been storing up with such glee that, during at least the period from when he first discovered it through the period up till now when he was about to reveal it, he was almost able to forget his larger troubles. If not now, when?, Burt figured, as he scratched out of his pocket a piece of paper on which he'd written a website address. Burt asked if anybody was available for a good laugh. He got a few takers but it wouldn't have mattered if the others had stared him to death. It was too good. It was too perfect. Burt said for everyone who had a pen or pencil to write down the website. A few did, most didn't, but it didn't matter really because Pete Hammond had his laptop with him. The whole breakfast crowd stuffed itself around

Pete and his laptop as if he were the Brigadiers' Frank Magglia about to explain a touchdown play. Pete laboriously copied the address into his browser and when he finally had it right, pressed return. The McDonald's wi-fi wasn't the swiftest, but after some seconds there appeared on the screen a promo for a new porn short, an internet exclusive, that if you wanted to see the good parts would cost you six ninety-five. But the trailer was sufficient, first promising the "return to action" of a gifted performer whose absence from the business had been missed, then fading to the kind of vacant California house traditional in porn productions, which looked to have nothing more to it than a pool and an empty refrigerator and, somewhere, eventually, a bed. Today the gas company guy was coming to check the meter. LynnieRae and her girlfriends were waiting for him. The title of the short appeared: "Billy's Willy." Then Billy Hutchins knocked on the door.

Bealport Days

Wednesdays now were Bealport Days at Big Jim's Surplus and Salvage, ten percent more off of everything. It was enough for a few of the girls to organize an expedition. Martha found a shower curtain that if it hadn't been returned to K-Mart on account of one of the eyelets being torn would have gone for sixteen dollars, but at Big Jim's was a dollar ninety-eight, and that was before the additional ten percent. The shower curtain had about sixteen eyelets so Martha figured they could surely live without one of them. Dawn stocked up on soap, big aloe bars that were smooth and shapely at fifty cents each, less the ten percent, so forty-five cents each. Bev Miles went down the men's shoe aisle, between the sizes ten to twelve, and discovered, crammed in towards the top of the high metal racks with horrible Brazilian slip-ons that looked to be woven out of cardboard and running shoes so clunky they defied anybody ever to run in them and lime green slippers from Malaysia that had no right or left foot, several pairs of the Norumbega cordovan monk straps, the ones she happened to know perfectly well retailed originally for three hundred ninety-five dollars, and here they were for twenty-two fifty, in this case counting the ten percent additional off. Burton took a 9 1/2 C shoe, which they didn't have, but they did have a 10D and a 9B and an 11C, and Bev decided to buy all of these, on the theory that Burton could at least try them on, and you never knew for sure with shoes, and she could always take them back. The seventy dollars or whatever it was was beyond her budget these days, but the shoes in their sturdy Norumbega boxes with the extra layers of tissue paper sealed with the little gold "N" seal reminded her, anyway, of Mikey.

In the parking lot she had the urge to see again what she had bought, and to show her friends. She removed the boxes from the oversized Toys 'R' Us bag that the checkout lady had placed them in. She laid the boxes on the hood of her Corolla and took the top off each box and delicately separated the layers of tissue paper from the little "N" seals and pushed the tissue paper aside so that the shoes could be seen. This was a moment when each of the women realized it would be best not to show as much emotion as she felt. Instead they all looked at what they had once been a part of making and silently seemed to agree, with slight nods, with surprised eyes, that these were too beautiful a part of life to let sit on Big Jim's metal shelves. Bev then offered the 11Cs to Martha, for Gary. But Gary wore a 12EE and Martha felt she had to say no thanks.

THE END